PASSING

MAURICE BARING

ZINC READ

Published by
This edition copyright © 2024 by Zinc Read
Design and setting By Zinc Read
Email- zincread@gmail.com
ISBN-978-93-6196-209-7

CONTENTS

PASSING BY

Friday, December 18th, 1908. Gray's Inn.

I went to the station this morning to see the Housmans off. They are leaving for Egypt and intend to stay there a month or perhaps two months. They are stopping a few days at Paris on the way.

Saturday, December 19th.

My Christmas holidays begin. I am spending Christmas with Uncle Arthur and Aunt Ruth. I have to be back at the office on the first of January.

Thursday, January 1st, 1909. Gray's Inn.

Received a post-card from Mrs Housman, from Cairo.

Monday, February 2nd.

Received a letter from Mrs Housman. They are returning to London.

Sunday, February 8th.

The Housmans return to-morrow. They have been away one month and twenty-one days.

Monday, February 9th.

Went to meet the Housmans at the station. They are going straight into their new house at Campden Hill and are giving a house-warming dinner next Monday, to which I have been invited.

Tuesday, February 10th.

Lord Ayton has been made Parliamentary Under-Secretary. I do not know him but I remain in the office. He is taking me on.

Monday, February 16th. Gray's Inn.

The Housmans had their house-warming in their new house at Campden Hill. I was the first to arrive.

On one of the walls in the drawing-room there is the large portrait of Mrs Housman by Walter Bell, which I had never seen since it was exhibited in the New Gallery ten years ago. It was always being lent for exhibitions when I went to the old house in Inverness Terrace. While I was looking at this picture Housman joined me and apologised for being late. He said the portrait of Mrs Housman was Bell's *chef-d'oeuvre*. He liked it *now.* Then he said: "We are having some music to-night. Solway is dining with us and will play afterwards. He plays for nothing here, an old friend; you know him? Miss Singer is coming too. You know her? She writes. I don't read her."

At that moment Mrs Housman came in and almost immediately Mr and Mrs Carrington-Smith were announced. Mr Carrington-Smith is Housman's partner, an expert in deep-breathing besides being rich. Mrs Carrington-Smith had lately arrived from Munich. The other guests were—Miss Housman (Housman's sister), Lady Jarvis, Miss Singer, whom I was to take in to dinner, a city friend of Mr Housman's, Mr James Randall, a little man with a silk waistcoat, and, the last to arrive, Solway. I sat on Mrs Housman's left, next to Miss Singer. Carrington-Smith sat on Mrs Housmans right; Housman sat at the head of the table, between Mrs Carrington-Smith and Lady Jarvis. Miss Singer talked to me earnestly at first. She is writing on the Italian Renaissance. I told her I was ignorant of the subject, upon which her earnestness subsided, and she smiled. Then we talked of music, where I felt more at home. She had been to all Solway's concerts. She is not a Wagnerite. Just as we were beginning to get on smoothly there was a shuffle in the conversation and Mrs Housman turned to me.

I told her we had a new chief at the office—Lord Ayton.

"We met him in Egypt," she said. "He had been big-game shooting. I had no idea he was an official."

I told her he was only a Parliamentary Under-Secretary. At that moment there was a lull in the general conversation and Housman overheard us.

"Ayton," he broke in. "A pleasant fellow, not too much money, some fine things, furniture, at his place, but he won't go far, no grit."

I asked Mrs Housman what he was like. She said they had made great friends at Cairo but she did not think they would ever meet again.

"You know," she said, "these great friends one makes travelling, people, you know, who are just passing by."

Miss Singer said he had an old house in Sussex. She had been over it. It was let; there were some fine old things there.

"But he won't sell," said Housman. "He's not a man of business."

Mrs Carrington-Smith said she preferred impressionist pictures, especially the Danish school. Housman laughed at her and said there was no money in them. Miss Housman said she had heard from a dealer that Lord Ayton had a remarkable set of Charles II. chairs and that she wished he would sell them. Solway took no part in the conversation but discussed music with Miss Singer. I caught the phrase, "trombones as good as Baireuth." Mrs Housman asked me whether I had seen Ayton yet. I told her he had not been to the office.

"I think you will like him," she said. Then, as an afterthought. "He's not a musician."

She asked me whether there were any changes in the staff. I told her none except for the arrival of a new Private Secretary (unpaid) whom Lord Ayton is bringing with him, called Cunninghame. She had never heard of him. We stayed a long time in the dining-room. Housman was proud of his Madeira and annoyed with us for not drinking enough. Mr Randall said he was sorry but he never mixed his wines, and he had some more champagne. Randall, Carrington-Smith and Housman talked of the international situation. Solway explained to me why portions of the Ninth Symphony were always played too fast. He was most illuminating. Then we went upstairs. More guests had arrived. A few people I knew, a great many I had not seen before, Solway played some Bach preludes and the Waldstein Sonata. The unmusical went downstairs. There were about a dozen people left in the drawing-room.

Afterwards there were some refreshments downstairs. I got away about half-past twelve.

Tuesday, February 17th. Gray's Inn.

Our first day under the new regime. The new chief came to the office to-day. He looks young, and was friendly and unofficial. The new Private Secretary came too, Mr Guy Cunninghame, an affable young man. He wears a beautifully tied bow tie. I wonder how it is done and whether it takes a long time or not. He is well dressed, but when it comes to describing him he is dressed like anyone else, and yet he gives the impression of being well dressed. I don't know why. I suppose it is an art like any other. I could not tie a tie like that to save my life. *Equidem non invideo magis miror.*

He seems to have been everywhere, to have read everything and to know everyone. He is not condescending, he is just naturally agreeable.

I had to go over to the Foreign Office in the morning to see someone in the Eastern Department. When I came back Cunninghame told me that a Mrs Housman had been to see Ayton, about some billet for her brother-in-law. She talked to him first. Cunninghame said he thought she did not like coming on such an errand. She then saw A., who said he would do what he could. He told C. afterwards he was sure he couldn't do anything for the fellow. C. had never met her nor heard of her, but curiously enough he said he recognised her from her picture which he had seen, Walter Bell's picture. I asked him if he had seen it at the New Gallery. He said no, at a dealer's in America two years ago.

I asked him if he was sure it was the same picture. He said he was quite sure. The picture was for sale.

"One couldn't mistake the picture," he said. "It's the best thing Walter Bell ever did. His pictures are valuable now he is dead, but there was a slump in them before he died, or rather, there never was a boom in them. That one picture attracted a great deal of attention when it was first exhibited, and then one heard little of him till he died. Now, of course, his pictures fetch high prices."

Letter from Guy Cunninghame to his cousin, Mrs Caryl

LONDON,

February 19*th*, 1909.

DEAREST ELSIE,

Since my last letter I have been installed. I am George Ayton's Secretary. I sit in the office with another man, who was there before and has been taken on, called Mellor. He is as silent as a deaf-mute and I have no doubt is the soul of discretion. There isn't much work to do and Ayton has got a real Secretary of his own who writes shorthand and typewrites without mistakes and lives in his house. He writes all his private letters and does all his business for him. He is not supposed to do official work, but George brings him to the office all the same, and he has a typewriter in the clerk's room and is always ready to do any odd job. I find him most useful. He is still more silent than Mellor. I haven't much to tell you. I have got into my new flat in Halkin Street. It will be presentable in time. The pictures are up, but not the curtains. Let us hope they won't be a failure: They were promised last week but have not yet arrived. If you have time and are passing that way I wish you would get me from the Bon Marché half-a-dozen coloured tablecloths.

George has got a flat in Stratton Street. I dined with him alone last night. We went to a Music Hall after dinner and heard Harry Lauder. His sister, Mrs Campion, is in Paris. Perhaps you will see her. Yesterday a lady came to the office to interview him and saw me first, a Mrs Housman. Have you ever heard of her? I recognised her at once as the subject of a picture by Walter Bell. Do you remember a large picture of a lady in white playing the piano? Such a clever picture. I saw it in New York at Altheim's shop, but I believe it was exhibited years ago at the New Gallery. Well, she is far more beautiful than the picture. She is not really tall, but she looks tall, with a wonderful walk, but I can't describe her, she makes other people look unreal—like wax-works. She was dressed anyhow and rather shabbily in black, wearing no gloves but the most beautiful ring I have ever seen, a kind of double monogram, probably old French. She came on business. I wonder who she is. She is not a foreigner and not, I think, an American, but she is, looks and talks, especially talks, not like an Englishwoman.

I shall try to come to Paris for Easter.

Don't forget the tablecloths.

Yours,

Guy.

From the Diary of Godfrey Mellor

Monday, March 1*st.*

I dined last night with the Housmans, They were alone except for Solway, and after dinner we had some music. Solway played the Schumann Variations and then he asked Mrs Housman to sing. I hadn't heard her for a long time as she hardly ever will sing now. She sang *Willst du dein Herz mir schenken*. Solway says the song isn't by Bach really but by his nephew. Then she sang a song from Purcell's *Dido*, some Schubert; among others, *Wer nie sein Brot*, and the *Junge Nonne*. Solway said he had never heard the last better sung. Housman then asked her to sing a song from *The Merry Widow*, which she did.

Housman plays himself by ear.

She did not allude to having been at the office, nor did I.

Tuesday, March 2*nd.*

Dined with Cunninghame at his flat last night. A comfortable and luxurious abode. I asked him if Ayton was likely to marry. He laughed. He said he had been in love for years, with a Mrs Shamier. I had never heard of her. Cunninghame said she was clever and accomplished, and had been very pretty and painted by all the painters.

He says A. will never marry. I asked him if Mrs Shamier was in London. He said of course. She has a husband who is in Parliament, and several children; a country house on the south coast; but they are not particularly well off.

"You must come and meet her at dinner," he said. "I am devoted to her."

I asked him if she was fond of A.

"Not so much now, but she won't let him go."

I went away early as C. was going to a party.

Wednesday, March 3rd.

Went to the British Museum before going to the office, to look up an old English tune for Mrs Housman from Ford's *Music of Sundry Kinds* called *The Doleful Lover*. I found it.

Thursday, March 4th.

Went to Solway's Chamber Music Concert last night.

Brahms Quintet and a trio by Solway himself. Some Brahms *Lieder*. The Housmans were there. I thought Solway's trio fine.

Friday, March 5th.

A. went to the country this afternoon to stay with the Shamiers; so C. said, but, as a matter of fact, he told me he was going to his own house. Cunninghame is going away himself to-morrow. He always goes away on Saturdays, he says. I remain in London.

Saturday, March 6th.

Went to the London Library and got some books for Sunday: *Thaïs*, by Anatole France, recommended to me by C.; a book called *A Human Document*, recommended me by Mrs Housman. I do not think I shall read any of them. The only literature I read without difficulty is *The Times* and *Jane Eyre*, and *The Times* doesn't come out on Sunday.

Sunday Night, March 7th.

Called on the Housmans in the afternoon. She was out. Luncheon at the Club. Dinner at the Club. I began *A Human Document*, but could not read more than five pages of it. I couldn't read any of the book by Anatole France.

Went to a concert in the afternoon. It was not enjoyable.

Read *Jane Eyre*.

Letter from Guy Cunninghame to Mrs Caryl

LONDON,

Monday, March 8th.

DEAREST ELSIE,

I meant to write you a long letter yesterday from the country. I went to stay with the Shamiers. I thought, of course, George would be there. He didn't come near the office on Friday. He wasn't there and evidently wasn't even expected.

Louise in tearing spirits and a new man there called Lavroff, a Russian philosopher; youngish and talking English better than any of us, except that he always said "I *have been* seeing So-and-so to-day," "I *have been to the concert yesterday*."

Needless to say, I didn't have a moment to write to you, in fact the only place where I get time to write you a line is at the office. Everything is appallingly dull. Mellor, the Secretary, had dinner with me one night. He spoke a little but not much. I think he is shy but not stupid.

George likes being in London, but Louise didn't mention him. It's curious if after all this fuss and trouble to get this job and to be in London it all comes to an end.

The tablecloths have arrived. Thank you a thousand times. They are exactly what I wanted. The curtains have arrived too but they are a failure; too bright. I can't afford to get new ones yet. This week I have got some dinners. George said something about giving a dinner this week.

Yours in great haste,

G.

From the Diary of Godfrey Mellor

Monday, March 8th.

A. asked me whether if I was free on Thursday I would dine with him. I said f would be pleased to. He said he would try and get a few people.

Tuesday, March 9th.

A. has got a Secretary called Tuke. He writes all his private letters and he comes down to the office in the mornings. This morning he came and asked me Mrs Housman's address. It is curious that he should have applied to me and not to C., as I was not here when she called, nor does A. know that I know her. How can he have known that I know her?

Wednesday, March 10th.

Dined with Cunninghame last night at his flat. The guests were Mr and Mrs Shamier, Miss Macdonald, C.'s cousin, M. Lavroff, a Russian, and a Miss Hope. I sat between the Russian and Miss Macdonald. Miss Macdonald is an elderly lady, kind and agreeable. Mr Shamier, M.P., was once, I believe, an athlete, a cricket Blue. Miss Hope looked as if she were in fancy dress; Lavroff, the Russian, is unkempt, with thick eyebrows and dark eyes. Tolstoy was mentioned at dinner. Mrs Shamier said he was her favourite novelist, upon which Lavroff became greatly excited and said the day would come when, the world would perceive and be ashamed of itself for perceiving that Tolstoy was not worthy to lick Dostoyevsky's boots. Being asked my opinion I was obliged to confess that I had read the works of neither novelist. Miss Macdonald asked me who was my favourite novelist. I said Charlotte Brontë. She said she shared my preference and couldn't read Russian books, they depressed her. After dinner we had some music. Miss Hope sang and accompanied herself. She sang songs by Fauré and Hahn; among others *La Prison*. She altered the text of the last line, and instead of singing "Qu'as tu fait de ta jeunesse?" she rendered it—"Qu'as tu fait dans ta jeunesse?": scarcely an improvement. When she had finished Lavroff was asked to play. He consented immediately and played some folk songs. Although he is in no sense a pianist, they were beautifully played.

Thursday, March 11*th.*

Had dinner last night with Admiral Bowes in Hyde Park Gardens. The only people there besides myself were Colonel Hamley and Grayson, who is, they say, a rising M.P. The Admiral said his nephew, Bowes in the F.O. (whom I know a little), had become a Roman Catholic.

"What on earth made him do that?" said Colonel Hamley.

"Got hold of by the priests," said the Admiral; and they all echoed the phrase: "Got hold of by the priests" and passed on to other topics.

I have often wondered what the process of being "got hold of by the priests" consists of, and where and how it happens.

Friday, March 12*th.*

Dined last night with A. at his flat. I was surprised to meet Mr and Mrs Housman. The hostess was A.'s sister, Mrs Campion. She is a deal older than he is, a widow and good company. There was also a Mrs Braham, and a younger man called Clive. He is in a bank and is, I believe, a useful man in a sailing boat.

I sat between Mrs Campion and Mrs Housman.

After dinner A. said to Mrs Housman that, knowing she liked music, he had provided her with a musical treat. Mrs Braham would sing to us. She sang, accompanying herself, *The Garden of Sleep, The Silver Ring, Mélisande in the Wood,* and, by special request, *The Little Grey Home in the West*. There was no other music.

Saturday, March 13*th.*

Had tea with the Housmans. They asked me to dinner next Tuesday to meet A. Mrs Housman says that Mrs Campion is one of the most charming and amusing people she has ever met. C. is staying in London. This Saturday A. is going to his house in the country. He has a small house on the coast near Littlehampton, where he keeps his yacht, but, of course, he cannot yacht yet. He has a large house in Sussex which is let.

Sunday Night, March 14*th.*

Went down to Woking to spend the day with Solway in his cottage. He is composing a Sonata for piano and violin. He played me the first movement. He said he thought there was a certain amount of good music being composed at the present day which nobody was taking notice of, but which would probably come into its own some day. He said Mrs Housman was the singer who gave him the most pleasure. He said: "Her singing is *business-like*. She is divinely musical."

Letter from Guy Cunninghame to Mrs Caryl

Sunday, March 14*th.*

DEAREST ELSIE,

I have been spending a perfect Saturday to Monday in London. I have had a busy week and was glad to see no one and do nothing all to-day, that is to say, comparatively no one and nothing, as I went to the play on Saturday night, and to-day I went to a large luncheon party at Alice's, who is back at Bruton Street. The news is that the Shamier episode is over, quite, quite over. There is no doubt about it. She is madly in love with Lavroff. I don't wonder. He is so intelligent and plays wonderfully. As for George, I don't think he cares. You will at once ask if there is no one else. Nobody that I know of. I don't know who he sees and what he does. He hates going out, and talks every day of giving a dinner at his flat, but as far as I know he hasn't entertained a cat yet.

I dined out every night last week, and gave one dinner at my flat. I think it was a success. Freda Macdonald, Louise, Lavroff and Eileen Hope, who sang quite beautifully. I asked Godfrey Mellor, but I really don't know if I can ask him again to that sort of party as he didn't utter a word. Freda liked him. But it does ruin a dinner to have a gulf of silence in the middle of it, especially as when he does talk he can be quite agreeable. George has gone down to the country. His sister is here now, but she goes north next week. I believe London bores him to death and he is longing for the summer and for his yacht. I am sorry you can tell me nothing of Mrs Housman. I haven't seen or heard anything more of her.

Thank you very much for the *langues de chat*. They added to the success of my dinner. Yours, etc.,

GUY.

From the Diary of Godfrey Mellor

Monday, March 16*th.*

I asked C. where he got his cigarettes. He said he got them from a little man who lived *behind* the Haymarket. Everybody seems to get their cigarettes and their shirts from a "little man." The little man apparently never lives in a street but always *behind* a street.

My new piano, a Cottage Broadwood, arrived to-day. It is bought on the three years' system.

Tuesday, March 17*th.*

Dined with my Aunt Ruth and Uncle Arthur last night, in Eccleston Square. A large dinner-party: a Permanent Under-Secretary for Foreign Affairs, the French Chargé d'Affaires and his wife, the Editor of *The Whig* and his wife, Lord and Lady Saint-Edith, Professor Miles, Sir Herbert

Wilmott and Lady Wilmott, Mr Julius K. Lee of the American Embassy, and Mrs Lovell-Smythies, the novelist.

As we were all waiting for dinner in the dark library downstairs a Miss Magdalen Cross came in late, carrying a book in her hand. "This book," she said to us all, "is well worth reading." It was a German novel by Sudermann. An old lady who was standing next to her, and who I afterwards discovered was the widow of the Bishop of Exminster, said: "You prepared that entry in your cab, dear Magdalen." Miss Cross blushed. I took her in to dinner. She talked of sculpture, the Chinese nation, German novels, and Russian music. She has been three times round the world. She has no liking for most German music and cannot abide Brahms. She likes Wagner, Chopin, Russian Church music and Spanish songs. On the other side I had the wife of the French Chargé d'Affaires. She said: "J'adore l'odeur des paquets anglais." Her favourite English author, she said, was Mrs Humphry Wood. I did not like to ask her if she meant Mrs Humphry Ward or Mrs Henry Wood. She said the works of this novelist made her weep.

When we were left in the dining-room after dinner, Lord Saint-Edith, Professor Miles and Hallam (of *The Whig*) had a long argument about some lines in Dante, and this led them to the Baconian theory. Lord Saint-Edith said he couldn't understand people thinking Bacon had written Shakespeare's plays. If they said Shakespeare had written the works of Bacon as a pastime he could understand it. He believed Homer was written by Homer. The Professor was paradoxical and said he thought the Odyssey was a forgery. "Tacitus," he said, "was known to be one."

After dinner upstairs there was tea but no music. Uncle Arthur is growing very deaf and forgetful and asked me how I was getting on at Balliol.

Aunt Ruth told me she had asked my new chief to dinner, but that he had refused. "Of course," she said, "this is not the kind of house he would find amusing. But considering how well I knew his father I think it would be only civil for him to come to one of my Thursday evenings."

Wednesday, March 17th.

I dined at the Housmans' last night. It was a dinner for A. He was the guest of the evening. To meet him there were Lady Maria Lyneham, who must be over seventy; a French lady of imposing presence called, if I caught the name correctly, the Princesse de Carignan and who, Housman whispered to me, was a Bourbon, and if she had her rights would be Queen of France to-day; a secretary from the Italian Embassy;

Mr and Mrs Baines. Mr Baines is an official at the British Museum and is half French. His wife, he told me, had once been taken for Sarah Bernhardt. There were several other people: Sir Herbert Simcox, the K.C., and Lady Simcox, an art critic, a lady journalist and Miss Housman.

A. sat between Mrs Housman and Lady Simcox. Housman had the Princesse de Carignan on his right and Lady Maria on his left. I sat between Lady Maria and Miss Housman. Lady Maria told me she dined out whenever she could, and asked me to luncheon on Sunday. "Don't come," she said, "if you mind meeting lions; I like pleasant people. Only I warn you I have an old-fashioned prejudice for good manners and I always ask their wives."

Mr Baines talked beautiful French to the Princesse. Lady Maria told me she was neither French nor a princess, but the illegitimate daughter of a Levantine. "But very respectable all the same, I'm afraid," she added.

After dinner a few people came. Among others, Housman's partner and Esther Lake, the contralto. She sang (she brought her own accompanist) some Handel and *Che faro* and, by request of Mr Housman, Gounod's *There is a Green Hill.*

I drove home with A. He told me he had enjoyed himself immensely and he thought Esther Lake was the finest singer in the world.

He said Miss Housman was a very clever woman and Housman appeared to be quite a good sort.

He said he liked this kind of dinner-party.

Thursday, March 18*th.*

The first day there has been a feeling of spring in the air. I went to St James's Park on the way to the office.

Dined at the Club.

Friday, March 19*th.*

A. asked me to spend Sunday with him in the country. I told him I was sorry I was engaged to go out to luncheon on Sunday. He said I must come the week after.

Saturday, March 20*th.*

C. said it was a great pity A. did not go out more. He used to go out a great deal, he said. "I suppose," he added, "it's because he doesn't wast to meet Mrs Shamier." I said I thought C. had told me he was fond of her. "Yes," said C, "he was very fond of her, but that is all over now."

*Sunday Evening, March 21*st.

I went to St Paul's Cathedral in the morning. Then to luncheon with Lady Maria in her house in Seymour Place.

A curious luncheon. There were two actors and their wives, Father Seton, and Mr Le Roy, who writes detective stories, and his wife, and Sir James Croker.

I sat next to Mrs Le Roy, who is, she told me, a Greek. She told me her husband had written one hundred and ten books, but that she had read none of them. She said it worried him if she read them. She said it was a great sacrifice as she doted on detective stories and was told his were very good. The actors, who were both actor managers, told us about their forthcoming productions. Mr Vane said there was going to be a real panther in his next production (a Shakespearean revival). Mr Jones Acre is producing a play which is translated from the Swedish, and which deals with the question of a man who has inoculated himself and his whole family with a fatal disease, in the interests of science.

Father Seton took a great interest in the stage, and said he considered the Church and the stage should be close allies. The clergy took far too little interest in these things. It was a pity, he said, to let the Romans have the monopoly of that kind of thing. This surprised Mrs Le Roy, who said she thought he was a Roman Catholic. He laughed and said Rome would have to capitulate on many points before any idea of corporate reunion could be entertained.

Sir James Croker told stories of early days in the Foreign Office and Lord Palmerston.

We sat on talking until half-past three. I then went home and read *Jane Eyre*.

Letter from Guy Cunninghame to Mrs Caryl

HALKIN STREET,

March 25th.

DEAREST ELSIE,

I start on Thursday and shall arrive Thursday evening. I have got rooms at the Ritz. Let us have dinner together Thursday night, and *not* go to a play. I shall stay in Paris a week and then go for four days to Mentone. Then I shall come back to Paris for three days, and then home. I suppose we shall have to dine at the Embassy one night. George is going to the country for Easter with his sister. I want a really nice screen (a small one). You must help me to find one, not too dear. I also want something for the dining-room, which at present is coo bare.

I won't write any more now.

Yours,

G.

From the Diary of Godfrey Mellor

Sunday, March 29th. Hôtel St Romain, Rue St Roch, Paris

Went to a concert at the *Cirque d'Été* this afternoon, not a very interesting programme. A great deal of Wagner, and *L'Après-midi d'un Faune.*

Dined by myself at a Duval. Start for Florence to-morrow morning.

Tuesday, March 30th. Villa Fersen, Florence

Arrived this morning before luncheon after an exhausting journey second-class. In the carriage there was a soldier belonging to the *Garde Républicaine.* He said he was on duty at the Opera and had he known I was passing through Paris he could have given me a *billet de faveur.*

The Housmans' villa is at the top of a hill on the Bellosguardo side. It is rather a large house, covered with wistaria, with high windows with iron bars. It has a large empty *salon* with a piano. A fine room for sound. The garden is beautiful.

Wednesday, March 31st.

I walked down into Florence very early in the morning. I reached the town before anything was open and met a party of men in shorts and flannels running back to a hotel. They were Eton masters taking exercise. I didn't go to any picture galleries, but I walked about the streets and went into the Duomo, an ugly building inside. I got back for luncheon.

Housman said that they must leave cards in the afternoon and take a drive in the Cascine. They went out in a carriage and pair. I went for a walk to the Boboli Gardens. At dinner Housman said they had met several friends, and he is giving a dinner-party on Sunday.

Thursday, April 1st.

The Housmans took me to luncheon with a banker called Baron Strong. What the explanation of this title is I do not know. They live in the modern part of the town. He was a genial host, portly, with long white whiskers. His wife, the Baroness, an Italian, a distinguished lady. There were present a Marchese whose real name I was told was Goldschmidt, and his wife, a retired and talkative English diplomatist, a Russian lady, an Italian, who talked English, French and Russian with ease, called Scalchi, Professor Johnston-Wright, who is spending his holiday here, and a Frenchman. When the latter heard Scalchi talk every language successively he said to him: "Vous êtes une petite tour de Babel."

In the afternoon we left cards at several houses and villas and then went for a drive in the Cascine. Some people called at tea-time, but I escaped. After dinner Mrs Housman sang some Schumann, *Frühlingsnacht*, and the *Dichterliebe.* These songs, she said, suit Florence.

Friday, April 2nd.

I had a talk with the Italian gardener as far as my Italian permitted me to. I pointed out a plant, a mauve-coloured plant, I don't know its name, that seemed to grow in great profusion. He said: "Fiorisce come il pensiere dell' uomo." More calls in the afternoon, and another drive in the Cascine.

Housman has bought a large modern statue representing *The Triumph of Truth,* a female figure carrying a torch, with a serpent at her feet. She is triumphing, I suppose, over the snake.

Saturday, April 3rd.

We went to see the Easter Saturday ceremony at the Duomo, and then to luncheon at the Villa Michael Angelo. It belongs to a rich American called Fisk. There were present besides Mr and Mrs Fisk an English authoress, a picture connoisseur, Scalchi, an American archæologist, an Italian man of letters, and a Miss Sinclair, also an archæologist. Housman said afterwards this was the cream of intellectual Florence.

I sat between two archæologists. I found their conversation difficult to follow.

After luncheon we called on the British Consul's wife, whose day it was. Then after a drive in the Cascine we went home.

Easter Sunday, April 4th.

Mrs Housman went to Mass early. Went for a walk with Housman. On the Ponte Vecchio we met Ayton and his sister, Mrs Campion. Mrs Campion, he said, had insisted on him taking her to Florence.

Housman asked them to dinner to-night; they accepted. A great many people came to tea.

The dinner-party to-night was quite a large one. Baron and Baroness Strong, Lord Ayton, Mrs Campion, Mr and Mrs Fisk, Scalchi and the Marchese and his wife, whom we met lately. I sat between Mrs Campion and Baron Strong. After dinner Mrs Fisk played Chopin with astonishing facility, but without any expression.

A. intends to stay here another fortnight.

Housman said he received a telegram which will necessitate his meeting his partner at Genoa. His partner is on the way to the Riviera. He may have to go to Paris too, but he hopes not, and intends to be back in a few days if possible.

Monday, April 5th.

Housman left to-day for Genoa. I went with Mrs Housman to San Marco and the Accademia in the morning. In the afternoon to the Certosa with Mrs Housman, A. and Mrs Campion.

Tuesday, April 6th.

Mrs Campion and A. came to luncheon. Mrs Campion, who is an expert gardener, told me the names of all the flowers in the garden. They have not remained in my mind.

Wednesday, April 7th.

We all spent a morning sight-seeing and had luncheon at a restaurant. In the afternoon we drove to Fiesole.

Thursday, April 8th.

Housman is not coming back. He is obliged to go to Paris and he will go straight to London from there.

We drove to Fiesole in the morning. Had luncheon with some Italian friends of Mrs Campion, Count and Countess Alberti. Nobody there except the host and hostess and their three children. A fine villa and no garden. Countess Alberti said it was no use having a garden if one lived here in summer, as everything dried up. She is a charming woman, natural and unpretentious, and talks English like an Englishwoman.

She asked A if he had met many people, and A. said he was a tourist and had no time for visits. Countess Alberti said he was quite right and that she knew nothing in the world more—*seccante* was the word she used, than Florentine society.

She asked us all to come again next week. I am leaving on Sunday, and A. and Mrs Campion are going to Paris on Monday. Mrs Housman remains here another week.

Friday, April 9th.

Mrs Housman had a headache and did not come down. I went to the town and did some shopping and went over the Bargello. Mrs Housman came down to dinner and sang afterwards, Schubert, Schumann and Brahms. I had never heard her sing *O Versenk o versenk dein Leid mein Kind, in die See* before.

Saturday, April 10th.

We went to a great many churches in the morning and saw a number of frescoes. Mrs Housman received a great many invitations, but refused them all. A. and Mrs Campion and the Albertis came to dinner. Countess Alberti persuaded Mrs Housman to sing. She sang some English songs: *Passing By, Lord Randall,* etc., Gounod's *Chanson de Mai,* and some Lully. Countess Alberti said it was a comfort to hear singing of which you could hear every word. A. liked *Passing By* best, and he made her sing it twice. He asked me who the words were by. The tune is Edward Purcell's. The words, although generally attributed to Herrick by musical publishers, are by an anonymous poet, and occur in Thomas Ford's *Music of Sundry Kinds*, 1607. They are as follows:—

There is a ladye sweet and kind,
Was never face so pleas'd my mind,
I did but see her passing by,
And yet I love her till I die.

Her gestures, motions, and her smile,
Her wit, her voice my heart beguile,
Beguile my heart, I know not why;
And yet I love her till I die.

There is also a third stanza.

Letters from Guy Cunninghame to Mrs Caryl

VILLA BEAU SITE,
MENTONE,
Thursday, April 8th.

DEAREST ELSIE,

It is divine here and this villa is a dream. We went to Monte Carlo yesterday and I won 300 francs and then lost it again. I saw hundreds of people, *monde* and *demi-monde*. Among the latter Celia Russell, having luncheon with rather a gross-looking shiny financier. I asked who he was and found out that he was Housman of Housman & Smith. Apparently C.R. has been living with him for some time, ever since, in fact, L. went to India. But the interesting thing to me is that Housman is the husband of that beautiful Mrs Housman I told you about. M. knows them and knows all about them. Mrs Housman was a Canadian, very poor, with no one to look after her but an old aunt. He married her about ten years ago. Since then he has become very rich. Carrington-Smith is now his partner. Housman supplies the brains. They live somewhere in the suburbs and she never goes anywhere.

I am not coming back till next Monday. I shall be able to stop two or three days in Paris, very likely longer.

Yours,
G.

HALKIN STREET,

Sunday, May 9th.

DEAREST ELSIE,

I have had a busy week since I have been back. Monday I dined with George at his flat. A man's dinner to meet some French politicians who are over here for a few days. I told you I was determined to make Mrs Housman's acquaintance, and I have. I had luncheon on Tuesday with Jimmy Randall, a city friend of mine. You don't know him. He knows the Housmans intimately. I told him I wanted to know them and he asked me to meet them last night.

We dined at the Carlton, Randall, the Housmans and myself. I think she is even more beautiful than I thought before. I couldn't take my eyes off her. She was in black, with one row of very good pearls. I never saw such eyes. Housman is too awful; sleek, fat and common beyond words, but sharp as a needle. He has an extraordinary laugh, a high, nasal chuckle, and says, "Ha! ha! ha!" after every sentence. They have asked me to dinner next Tuesday. I will write to you about it in detail. Mrs H. is charming. There is nothing American or Colonial about her, but she is curiously un-English. I can't understand how she can have married him. I caught sight of her again this morning at the Oratory, where I always go if I am in London on Sundays, for the music. Randall told me she is very musical, but I didn't get any speech with her.

The flat looks quite transformed with all the Paris things. They are the greatest success.

Yours,

G.

Wednesday, May 12th.

DEAREST ELSIE,

The dinner-party came off last night. They live in Campden Hill. I was early and the parlour-maid said Mrs Housman would be down directly, and I heard Housman shouting upstairs: "Clare, Clare, guests," but he did not appear himself. I was shown into a large white and heavily gilded drawing-room, with a candelabra, a Steinway grand, and light blue satin and ebony furniture, a good many palms, but no flowers. The drawing-room opened out on to an Oriental back drawing-room with low divans, small stools inlaid with mother-of-pearl, and a silver lamp (from a mosque) hanging from the ceiling, heavy curtains too, behind which I suspect stained-glass windows. Over the chimney-piece an Alma Tadema (a group on a marble seat against a violet sea). At the other end of the room Walter Bell's picture. It *was* the picture I saw before, but more about that later. On another wall over a sofa a most extraordinary allegorical picture: a precipice bridged by a large serpent, and walking on the serpent two small figures, a woman in white draperies and a knight dressed like Mephistopheles, all these painted in the crudest colours. The Housmans then appeared, and Housman did the honours of the pictures, faintly damned the Alma Tadema, and said the Snake Picture was by Mucius of Munich in what he called *Moderne* style. He had picked it up for nothing; some day it would be worth pots of money. Ha! ha! Then the guests arrived. Sir Herbert Simcox, K.C., Lady Simcox, dressed in amber velvet and cairngorms; Housman's sister Miss Sarah, black, and very large, in yellow satin, with enormous emerald ear-rings; Carrington-Smith, Housman's partner; Mrs Carrington-Smith, naked except for a kind of orange and red *Reform Kleid*, with a green complexion, heavily blacked eyebrows, and a *Lalique* necklace. Then, making a late entrance, as if on the stage, a Princesse de Carignan, a fine figure, in rich and tight black satin and a large black ruff, heavily powdered. Housman whispered to me that she was a legitimate Bourbon. I think he meant a Legitimist. We went down to dinner into a dark Gothic panelled dining-room, with a shiny portrait of Mr Housman set in the panelling over the chimney-piece.

I sat between Mrs Housman and Mrs Carrington-Smith. I talked to Mrs Housman most of the time. Mrs Carrington-Smith asked me if I liked Henry James's books. I said I liked the early ones. She said she preferred the later ones, but she could never feel quite the same about Henry James again since he had put her into a book. She was, she said, *Kate* in *The Wings of the Dove*. After dinner Housman moved up and sat next to me. He talked about art and *bric-à-brac*. I asked him if I could possibly have seen Bell's portrait of Mrs Housman in America. He said, "Certainly." He had bought it cheap and sold it dear, anticipating a slump in Bell, which was not slow in coming. He had then bought it back directly Bell died, anticipating a boom, which had also occurred. "It is now worth double what I gave for it. Ha! ha! ha!"

Randall said he liked a picture to tell a plain story and he could make nothing of the Snake Picture upstairs. Housman laughed loudly and said it was the oldest story in the world: the man, the woman, and the serpent. Ha! ha! We went upstairs, where there was a crowd. I was seized upon by the Princesse de Carignan, and she whispered to me confidential secrets about Europe. She preened herself and displayed the deportment of a queen in exile.

Then we had some music. Esther Lake bawled some Rubinstein, and Ronald Solway played an interminable sonata by Haydn with variations and all the repeats. Some of the guests went downstairs, but I was wedged in between the Princesse and a Mrs Baines, a fluffy, sinuous woman, dressed in a loose Byzantine robe. Her husband, who is an expert in French furniture, told me she was once mistaken for *Sarah*, and she has evidently been living up to the reputation for years. He was careful to add that it was in the days when Sarah was thin—Mrs Baines being a wisp.

After the music, which I thought would never stop, we went downstairs again for a stand-up supper and sweet champagne. I was introduced by Housman to Ronald Solway. Housman told him I was a musical connoisseur, so he bored me with technicalities for twenty minutes. I couldn't get away. He had no mercy on me. Housman has got a box at the Opera. He told me I must use it whenever I like. How can she have married that man?

Yours,

G.

Wednesday,
May 19*th*.

DEAREST ELSIE,

Thank you for your most amusing letter. I have been busy and not had a moment to write. We have had a good deal of work to do. Last Friday I had supper at Romano's after the play. Housman was there with Celia Russell. I spent Saturday to Monday with the Shamiers. Lavroff was there. Last night I went to the Opera to the Housmans' box. It was *Bohème*. During the *entr'acte* who should come into our box but George. He stayed there the whole time, talking to Mrs H., and came back during the next *entr'acte*.

The next day at the office when I was in his room I said something about the Housmans and began telling him about my dinner. He froze at once and said Mrs Housman was an extremely nice woman. I said something about Housman, and George said: "Oh, not at all a bad fellow." So I saw I was on dangerous ground. Housman has asked me to spend next Sunday at his country house, a small villa on the Thames near Staines. I am going.

They are dining with me on Thursday. I asked George, too, and he accepted joyfully.

Yours,

G.

Monday, May 24*th.*

DEAREST ELSIE,

I am just back from the country. But first I must tell you about my dinner. I had asked the Housmans, George, Eileen Hope, and Madame de Saint Luce who is staying in London for three weeks. Just before dinner I got a telegram saying that Mrs Housman was laid up and couldn't possibly come. Housman arrived by himself. George was evidently frightfully annoyed and hardly spoke. Madame de Saint Luce was amazed and rather amused by Housman, and after dinner Eileen sang beautifully, so it went off fairly well except for George.

Saturday I went down to Staines. Housman had got an elegant villa on the river. Very ugly, with red tiles, photogravures, and green wooden chairs and a conservatory, full of calceolaria. But I must say his food is delicious. George was there, Lady Jarvis, and Miss Sarah.

After dinner on Saturday there was a slight fracas. George asked Mrs Housman to sing. She didn't much want to, but finally said she would. Miss Sarah, who is a brilliant pianist, said she would accompany her (she evidently hates being accompanied). She sang a song of Schubert's, *Gute Nacht*. Miss Sarah played it rather fast. Mrs Housman said it ought to be slower. Miss Sarah said it was meant to be fast, and that was her conception of the song in any case.

Mrs Housman said she couldn't sing it like that, and didn't, and then she said she couldn't sing at all. Afterwards she did sing some English ballads and accompanied herself.

She sings most beautifully, her voice is perfectly produced and you hear every word. There is nothing throaty or operatic about it but her voice goes straight through one. George was entranced. Sunday afternoon George and Mrs H. went out on the river and stayed out all the afternoon. I spent the afternoon with Lady Jarvis, who is most clever and amusing. She told me all about the Housmans. Mrs H. is not Canadian but Irish. She was brought up in a convent in French Canada. Directly she came out of it her marriage with H., who was then in a Canadian firm, was arranged by her aunt (her aunt was an imbecile and quite penniless). They lived several years in Canada, California and other parts of America, and came to England about three years ago. Housman was unfaithful from the first. Lady Jarvis knew about Celia Russell. I asked her if Mrs Housman knew. She said she—Lady Jarvis—didn't know, but it wouldn't make any difference if Mrs H. did or not. She said: "There is nothing about Albert Housman that Clare doesn't know." Then she said that unless I was blind I must of course have seen George was madly in love with her.

I said I agreed. She said she thought Mrs Housman was madly in love with him. I said I wasn't sure. Lady Jarvis said she was quite sure.

They came back very late from the river and Mrs Housman didn't come down to dinner. She said she had a headache. We had rather a gloomy dinner although Miss Sarah and Lady Jarvis never stopped talking for a moment, but George was silent.

You know he sees nobody now except the Housmans.

Yours,

G.

From the Diary of Godfrey Mellor

Monday, May 3rd. Gray's Inn.

A. returned to London a day sooner than he was expected. His Secretary, Tuke, had not returned. He had left his address with me. He spent his holiday in the Guest House, Fort Augustus Abbey, a Benedictine monastery. He returned this morning. A. asked me on Saturday where he was. When I told him, A. showed great surprise. He said: "He has been with me six years and I never knew he was an R.C. It's extraordinary when a thing once turns up, you then meet with it every day. I seem always to be coming across Catholics now."

Tuesday, May 4th.

Alfred Riley telegraphed to me to know whether I could put him up to-night. I have answered in the affirmative, but he will be, I fear, most uncomfortable.

Wednesday, May 5th.

Riley arrived last night. He has been in Paris for the last three months working at the *Bibliothèque Nationale*. He told me he had something of importance to tell me: that he was seriously thinking of becoming a Roman Catholic. I was greatly surprised. He was the last person I would expect to do such a thing. I told him I had no prejudice against Roman Catholics, but it was very difficult for me to believe that a man of his intellectual attainments could honestly believe the things he would be expected to believe. Also, if he needed a Church I did not understand why he could not be satisfied with the Church of England, which was a historic Church. He said: "Do you remember when we were at Oxford that we used to say it would be a great sell if we found out when we were dead that Christianity was true after all? Well, I believe it is true. I believe, not in spite of my reason, nor against my reason, nor apart from my reason, but with my reason. Well, if one believes with one's reason in the Christian revelation, that is to say, if one believes that God has uttered Himself fully and uniquely through Christ, such a belief has certain logical consequences." I said nothing, for indeed I did not know what to say. Riley laughed and said: "Don't be alarmed; don't think I am going to hand you a tract. For Heaven's sake let me be able to speak out at least to one person about this." I begged him to go on, and he said he thought Catholicism was the only logical consequence of a belief in the Christian revelation. Anglicanism and all forms of Protestantism seemed to him like the lopped off branches of a living tree.

I asked him what there was to prevent him worshipping in Roman Catholic churches if he felt inclined that way without sacrificing his intellectual freedom to their tenets.

He said: "You talk as if it was ritual I cared for and wanted. One can be glutted with ritual in the Anglican Church if one wants that."

As for giving up one's freedom, he said I must agree that law, order and discipline were the indispensable conditions of freedom. He had never heard Catholics complain of any loss of freedom, indeed Catholic philosophy, manners, customs, and even speech, seemed to him much freer than Protestant or Agnostic philosophy, and what it stood for. He asked me which I thought was freest, a Sunday in Paris or Rome or a Sunday in Glasgow or London.

I suggested his waiting a year. He said perhaps he would.

Thursday, May 6th.

Riley talked of music, Wagner, *Parsifal.* He quoted some Frenchman who said that *Parsifal* was "*moins beau que n'importe quelle Messe Basse dans n'importe quelle Église.*" I said that I had never been to a Low Mass in my life, but that I disliked the music at most High Masses I had attended. I said I disliked Wagner, especially *Parsifal*. He said he agreed about Wagner, but I did not understand what the Frenchman had meant. I confessed I did not. He said: "It is like comparing a description of something to the reality." I told him that I envied people who were born Catholics, but I did not think it was a thing you could become. He said it was not like becoming a Mussulman. He was simply going back to the older tradition of his country, to what Melanchthon and Dr Johnson called and what in the Highlands they still call the Old Religion. I told him that I had once heard a man say, talking of becoming a Roman Catholic, "if I could tell the first lie, all the rest would be easy and follow naturally down to scapulars and Holy Water."

Friday, May 7th.

Riley left this morning. He has gone back to Paris. He is not going to take any immediate step.

Sunday, May 9th

I went to see Mrs Housman yesterday afternoon. I told her what Riley had told me. I asked her if she thought people could *become* Roman Catholics if they were not born so. She said she wished that she had not been born a Catholic so as she might have become one. She envied those who could make the choice. I asked her if she did not consider there was something unreal about converts. She said she thought English converts were in a very difficult situation which required the utmost tact. Many perhaps lacked this tact. She said that in Canada and America, where she had lived most of her life, the anti-Catholic prejudice as it existed in England did not exist, at any rate it was not of the same kind. "The nursery anti-Catholic tradition doesn't exist there."

She asked me what I had advised Riley to do. I told her I had dissuaded him from taking such a step and had begged him to wait. She said: "If he is to become a Catholic there will be a moment when he will not be able to help it. Faith is a gift. People do not become Catholics under the influence of people or books, although people and books may sometimes help or sometimes hinder, but because they are pulled over by an invisible rope—-what we call *Grace*."

I told her I would find it difficult to believe that a man like Riley would believe what he would have to believe. She asked me whether I found it difficult to believe that she accepted the dogmas of the Church. I said I was convinced she believed what she professed, but that I thought that born Catholics believed things in a different way than we did. I did not believe that this could be learnt by converts.

She said I probably thought that Catholics believed all sorts of things which they did not believe. Such at least was her experience of English Protestants, who seemed to imbibe curious traditions in the nursery, on the subject.

I asked her if Mr Housman believed in Catholic dogma. She said: "Albert has been baptized and brought up as a Catholic, but he is an Agnostic. He is very charitable towards Catholic institutions."

She asked me more about Riley and whether he had any Catholic friends. I said: "Not to my knowledge." "Poor man, I am afraid he will be very lonely," she said.

She said that she herself knew hardly any Catholics in England, that is to say she had no real Catholic friends, and that she felt as if she were living in perpetual exile.

"You see," she said, "your friend ought to realise that he will have to face the prejudice and the dislike not only of narrow-minded people but of very nice intelligent and broad-minded people, who agree with you about almost everything else. The Church has always been hated from the beginning, and it always will be hated. In the past it was people like Marcus Aurelius who carried out the worst persecutions and hated the Church most bitterly with the very best intentions, and it is in a different way just the same now."

I said that to me it was an impossible mental gymnastic to think that Catholicism was the same thing as early Christianity.

She said: "Because the tree has grown so big you think it is not the same plant, but it is. When I go to Mass I feel as if I were looking through the wrong end of a telescope right back into the catacombs and farther."

I told her Riley would take no decisive step. He had promised to wait. She said there was no harm in that. There were many other things I wished to ask her, but A. arrived, and after talking on various topics for a few moments I left.

Monday, May 10th.

A. told me he had been invited to dinner by Aunt Ruth next Thursday and that he was going. He asked me whether I was invited. I said I was invited.

Tuesday, May 11th.

Cunninghame said he was dining at the Housmans' to-night.

Wednesday, May 12th.

I asked C. whether he had enjoyed his dinner. He said it was very pleasant, but that the music was too classical for his taste. A. was not there.

Thursday, May 13th.

I dined last night with A. in his flat. Nobody but ourselves. A. played the pianola after dinner. He said I must come and stay with him in the country soon. He would try and get the Housmans to come too.

Friday, May 14th.

A. dined with Uncle Arthur and Aunt Ruth. So did I. It was a dinner for the American Ambassador. I sat next to a Miss Audrey Bax, a lady of decided views and picturesque appearance. She talked about Joan of Arc, and asked me whether I had read Anatole France's book about her. I said I had not, but I had read an English translation of Joan of Arc's trial which I thought one of the most impressive records I had ever read. She said: "Ah, you like the stained-glass-window point of view about those sort of people." I was rather nettled and said I preferred facts to fiction. I thought Joan of Arc as she appeared in her trial was a very sensible as well as being a very remarkable person. She had not read this. She said Anatole France told one all one wanted to know from a rational point of view. It was a comfort to read common-sense about this sort of hallucinated people. A man who was sitting opposite her joined eagerly in the conversation, and said that the two people in the whole of history who had made the finest defence when tried were Mary Queen of Scots and Joan of Arc. Miss Bax said she supposed he looked upon Mary Queen of Scots as a martyred saint. The other man, whose name I found out afterwards was Ashfield, an American who is now at the American Embassy, said that he regarded Mary Queen of Scots as a woman who was tried for her life and who had defended herself without lawyers without making a single mistake under the most difficult circumstances. He said he had been a lawyer, and spoke from a lawyer's point of view. Miss Bax went back to Joan of Arc and Anatole France and said his book was as important a work as Renan's *Vie de Jésus*. Mr Ashfield said he thought that work no improvement on the Gospel. I said I had not read it. Miss Bax again said that if we preferred sentimental traditions we were at liberty to do so. She preferred rational writers untainted by superstition. Ashfield said he regarded Renan as a sentimental writer. Miss Bax said: "No doubt you prefer Dean Farrar." Ashfield said he did not think Renan's book was a more successful attempt to rewrite the Gospels than Dean Farrar's although it was better written. She said that proved her point, and as she seemed satisfied, we talked of other things. But throughout her conversation she struck me for a professed free-thinker to be singularly dogmatic and sometimes almost fanatical.

Saturday, May 15th.

Spent the afternoon and evening with Solway at Woking but came back after dinner.

Sunday, May 16th.

Went to see Mrs Housman in the afternoon, but she was not at home. This is the first time she has not been at home on Sunday afternoons for a very long time.

Monday, May 17th.

A. said he was going to the opera to-night. Housman, whom he had seen yesterday, had told him it would be a very fine performance.

Tuesday, May 18th.

Went to the opera in the gallery. Some fine singing. Cunninghame had been in the Housmans' box.

Wednesday, May 19th.

Was going to dine with the Housmans to-night, but Mrs Housman is unwell.

Thursday, May 20th.

Lady Jarvis has asked me to stay with her Sunday week.

Friday, May 21st.

This morning a man called Barnes came to the office. He is an acquaintance of Cunninghame's; he is in the F.O. He talked of various things, and then he asked Cunninghame whether he knew Mrs Housman. He said she was playing fast and loose with A.'s affections. She was doing it, of course, to convert him. Catholics didn't mind how immoral they were in such a cause. He said that she was well known for it. She had refused to marry Housman till he had been converted. He had been so much in love with her that he could not refuse. I said that I happened to know that Housman had been baptized a Catholic when he was born. Cunninghame bore me out and said it was all nonsense about A. He was sure Catholicism had nothing to do with it. He knew Mrs Housman quite well and she had never mentioned it to him. Barnes said we could say what we liked, but all London was talking of A.'s unfortunate passion and Mrs H.'s behaviour.

"One sees them everywhere together," he said.

C. said: "Where?"

Barnes said: "Oh, at all the restaurants and at the opera."

Cunninghame said he had expected Mrs Housman to dinner, but she had been unable to come.

Saturday, May 22nd.

Called on Mrs Housman to inquire. They have gone to the country until Monday.

Monday, May 24th.

I had luncheon with A. to-day at his flat. He said he had been staying with the Housmans at their house on the Thames. He said he had put his foot in it. On Saturday night at dinner they were talking about Ireland, and he said he had no wish to go to a country full of priests. Mrs Housman told him, laughing, she was a Catholic. He asked me if I had known this. I told him I had always known it. He asked me whether she was very devout. I said I knew she always went to Mass on Sundays, that she had never mentioned the subject to me except once when I asked her a question with reference to a friend of mine. He asked me whether Housman was a Catholic too. I told him what I knew.

Tuesday, May 25th.

Went to the opera, in the Housmans' box. Housman and Cunninghame were there. Mrs Housman did not come. A. looked in during the *entr'acte*.

Wednesday, May 26th.

A. gave a dinner at his Club. All politicians except myself and Cunninghame.

Thursday, May 27th.

Tuke asked me to take a ticket for a concert at Hammersmith at which his sister is performing on the piano. I have done so.

Friday, May 28th.

Luncheon with A. at his Club. He is staying with Lady Jarvis on Saturday. The Housmans, he said, will be there. Cunninghame is going also. A. told me Mrs Housman has not been well lately. I said I thought she did too much. He asked me in what sort of way. I said she attended to a great many charities and that as Housman entertained a great deal I thought it tired her. Mrs Housman had told him I was very musical. He asked me if I played any instrument. I said none except the penny whistle. He asked me if I did not think Mrs Housman a very fine singer. I said I did. He also said that he supposed she knew a lot of priests. I said I had never met one in her house.

Sunday, May 30th. Rosedale, Surrey.

I arrived rather late last night. Besides the guests I knew I was to meet, was a Frenchman, M. Raphael Luc, and a Mrs Vaughan. After dinner we had some music. M. Luc sang several French songs, by Lully, and others that I had heard Mrs Housman sing. His singing was greatly appreciated and applauded, and it is, I confess, as far as it goes, perfection itself, as regards quality, taste and art, but I could not help thinking the whole time that it would be impossible for him to interpret Schubert.

This morning I sat in the garden and read the newspapers. Mrs Housman drove to Church which was some distance off.

Mr Winchester Hill, the novelist, arrived for luncheon and brought with him Miss Ella Dasent, the actress. At the end of the meal she gave us some vivid impersonations of contemporary actors and actresses.

We sat talking for some time in the verandah. Then Lady Jarvis took Housman to show him the garden, and Cunninghame walked away with Mrs Vaughan and M. Luc.

Miss Housman, Mr Hill, Miss Dasent, and myself remained on long chairs underneath a large tree. Miss Dasent and Mr Hill discussed at great length a play that he is adapting for her from one of his novels. The story seemed to me absurd—it was something about an Italian nobleman strangling his wife's lover with a silk handkerchief.

Towards five we had tea and after tea Mrs Vaughan took me for a stroll round the garden.

I found her a well-read woman who has lived a great deal in Paris and is familiar with the Bohemian world in more than one continent.

At dinner I sat between Mrs Housman and Cunninghame. Mrs Housman said that Luc's singing made one despair, and she felt she could never sing again after hearing him. I told her I doubted if he could interpret German music. She was annoyed with me and said I was missing the point, and that the songs he sang were exquisite.

We sat in the verandah after dinner, while Luc sang to us from the drawing-room. He sang Fauré's settings to Verlaine's words.

Letter from Guy Cunninghame to Mrs Caryl

Monday, May 21*st.*

DEAREST ELSIE,

I have just come back from Rosedale, where I have been staying with Lady Jarvis. It is an old Tudor house that was bodily transported from the west of England. I believe it is quite genuine, but it looks unreal and the rooms are like show rooms at a second-hand dealer's. The garden is quite beautiful. We had a most amusing party. Jane Vaughan (looking very pretty), Raphael Luc, George, the Housmans. Raphael sang both nights quite divinely after dinner. On Saturday night we all sat in the big downstairs room, but after he had sung two songs Mrs Housman went out on the verandah. She is so musical that one could see it was more than she could bear. I am certain she felt she was going to cry. Sunday morning I had a long talk with Lady Jarvis. She told me Mrs Housman is a very strict and devout Catholic. We both agreed that there is no doubt that George is very much in love with her. She thinks she *is* in love with him. I am still not sure Lady Jarvis is right about her. I sat next to her (Mrs H.) at dinner on Saturday night, and George was on her other side. She was perfectly natural, but I thought miles *away*. During the whole time we were there she didn't pay much attention to him and she didn't avoid him. She went to church by herself on Sunday morning and stayed in all the afternoon. I think she likes him, but nothing more than that.

Godfrey Mellor, the silent Secretary, is devoted to her too. The other morning at the office a man came to see us and said all sorts of most absurdly silly things about Mrs H. I could see he was furious. He has known the Housmans quite a long time.

More people came down to luncheon on Sunday, but nobody interesting. George says he will be able to yacht now. I think Mrs H. is delightful. I like her more and more. I have been to the opera twice, to a good many dinners, and some balls. There may be a chance of Paris for a few days later.

Yours,

G.

From the Diary of Godfrey Mellor

Monday, May 31st.

I travelled back from Rosedale with A. He asked me if I was fond of yachting. I said I was a moderate sailor. He asked me to go next Saturday to his house near Littlehampton. His sister is going to be there, and perhaps the Housmans. Dined at the Club.

Tuesday, June 1st.

There is going to be a large concert at the Albert Hall for the Albemarle Relief Fund. Tuke brought the programme and placed it on my table this morning. Esther Lake is singing, and the Housmans and A. are among the patrons. Dined with A. at his Club. He told me he thought Mrs Housman was far from well. He said what she wants is sea air.

Wednesday, June 2nd.

Cunninghame told me he had dined at the Housmans' last night. He said there was no one there but himself and Carrington-Smith. He said Mrs Housman talks of going away soon. London tires her. Dined at the Club.

Thursday, June 3rd.

I have just come back from a dinner-party at Aunt Ruth's. A great many diplomats and politicians. I sat between Thornton-Davis, who is at the F.O. now, and Mrs Vernon, who is French and a Legitimist and talks of the Place de la Concorde as the *Place Louis XV*. Aunt Ruth said she heard A. was doing very well and spoke well in the House. It's a pity, she said, that he is such a Tory.

Friday, June 4th.

Went this afternoon to the concert at the Albert Hall for the Relief Fund in the Housmans' box. Miss Housman and Mrs Carrington-Smith were there, but neither Mrs nor Mr Housman. Miss Housman says that Mrs Housman has not been well lately. She said she goes out far too much. I enjoyed nothing in the programme. Dined at the Club.

Saturday, June 5th.

A. told me he expected me at Littlehampton, but that I would find it dull, as he had no party.

Sunday, June 6th. Littlehampton.

A. has a nice and comfortable little house. His yacht, a small cutter with room for two to sleep on board, is here. He took Mrs Campion and myself out this morning. There was what is called a nice breeze. I cannot say I enjoyed it very much. He told me that he had asked the Housmans, but they could not come, Mrs Housman is going to Cornwall soon for the rest of the summer. She has not been well, and the doctors told her she must leave London. A. said he would miss them very much. He liked them both exceedingly, and he thought Miss Sarah was such a good sort. A. said the truth was that Mrs H. worked herself to death over charities and things like that. He was sure the priests were greatly to blame for this.

Letters from Guy Cunninghame to Mrs Caryl

LONDON,

Monday, June 7th.

DEAREST ELSIE,

There's not the slightest chance of my coming over to Paris now. I am not going to Ascot at all this year. The Housmans thought of taking a house for Ascot week, but she has not been well, and they are staying out of London till they go down to Cornwall. They have taken a house somewhere near the Lizard, and when she goes she will stay the whole summer.

Both George and poor little Mellor are in low spirits. I had a very nice letter from Mrs H. asking me to go down there in August and to stay as long as I liked.

Housman has lent me his box for the whole of Ascot week. There is such a rush that I haven't time to write properly to you.

Yours,

G.

LONDON,

Friday, June 18th.

DEAREST ELSIE,

I have spent the most perfect Ascot week in London. I have enjoyed every moment of it. I went to the opera every night in the Housmans' box, which besides being fun was most convenient as I was able to ask people who had done things for me. I dined on Saturday with Jimmy Randall, who had been at Ascot all the week. He says that Housman has fallen violently in love with a Mrs Rachel Park. You may possibly have heard of her. She used to sing at concerts under the name of Rose Sinclair. She was quite beautiful, with enormous eyes and flaming hair, but quite brainless and quite unmusical. She married a barrister who is now Park, K.C. He works like a slave, but she spends money more quickly than he can make it. This explains the Cornwall arrangement.

Jimmy R. says that H. has violent scenes with Celia R. and that the end of that idyll is only a question of hours. He says Mrs P. will lead him a dance. She is mercenary, stupid, common and a real harpy. Poor "Bert," as Jimmy Randall calls Housman. He is so good-natured. And poor Mrs H.! Mellor hardly speaks at all now, and George doesn't say much. He goes nowhere, but talks of yachting on the west coast during the summer.

Yours,

G.

P.S.—Just got your telegram. I am delighted you are coming to London. I particularly wanted you to meet Mrs Housman—and "Bert." You must come. And now I shall just be able to manage this if you will dine with me on Monday night. She leaves for Cornwall on Tuesday morning. I've asked George too. He stays in London till Parliament is over, and then he is going away and I shall be free. How much leave will Jack get? Three weeks at least, I hope. The Shamiers want you to stay with them Sunday week, and Lady Jarvis wants you to go down there. If you don't want to stay there, we might go down for luncheon one day. I shall be in London till the end of July. Then I am going to Worsel for a fortnight. The Housmans have asked me to go to Cornwall, and I shall try and fit that in between Worsel and the Shamiers. They have been lent a lodge in Scotland and have asked me to go there in September. I have promised to stay a few days at Edith's as well.

There is a parcel for me at the Embassy. It is too big for the bag. Could you bring it with you?

From the Diary of Godfrey Mellor

Tuesday, June 10*th.*

Dined with Cunninghame last night to meet his cousin, Mrs Caryl. She is the wife of a diplomat who is Second Secretary at Paris. A pleasant dinner. The Housmans were there, and A. and his sister.

Friday, June 25*th.*.

Received a letter from Mrs Housman to-day. She says the change of air is doing her good. She hopes I will come to Cornwall some time during my holiday.

Monday, July 5*th.*

Dined with Housman last night. Miss Housman was there, and the Carrington-Smiths, and a Mrs Park who used to be a professional singer. She sang after dinner. Miss Housman accompanied her. She sang Tosti's *Ninon,* some Lassen, some Bemberg, a song by Lord Henry Somerset, and E. Purcell's *Passing By*. Miss Housman said it was a comfort to accompany someone who had a sense of time. She has a powerful voice and has been well trained, but *Passing By* did not suit her style of singing, and I regretted that she had attempted that song. She was not always in tune.

Housman enjoyed it, and accompanied her himself afterwards in some coon songs which he played by ear.

Housman asked me to stay with them for the whole of August. He said he was very anxious that I should go, as he would not be able to be much in Cornwall and he was afraid Mrs Housman would be lonely. He asked Cunninghame also. I accepted.

A. spends all his spare time now on his yacht. I am going to stay with him next Saturday.

Monday, July 12th.

A. is going to the Cowes Regatta. He asked me to go with him, but I am leaving on the 1st of August for Cornwall.

Sunday, August 1st. Grey Farm, Carbis Bay, Cornwall.

I arrived here last night. A pleasant spot near the sea and not far from a golf links. Mrs Housman and Housman are here alone. Housman is greatly perturbed because Mrs Carrington-Smith is bringing a divorce suit against her husband for infidelity. The other person concerned is Miss Hope, whom I met at dinner one night at Cunninghame's flat. Housman says that Miss Hope is neurotic and unhinged. Mrs Housman has never met Miss Hope.

Housman said he hoped I would be able to stay on here, as he would not be able to spend much time in Cornwall. Carrington-Smith was so greatly upset by this wretched business that he could not attend to the affairs of the firm. He was afraid Mrs Housman would be lonely. Lady Jarvis had promised to come later, and Cunninghame also, but he did not know when. Miss Housman had been obliged to go to Vichy to take the waters. Housman played golf in the afternoon with a member of the Club. I am not a golf player, unfortunately. I told him that Cunninghame was an admirable player.

Monday, August 2nd.

Housman has been telegraphed for and left this morning. In the afternoon we went for a long drive and had tea in a farm-house. The climate is warm and agreeable.

Tuesday, August 3rd.

Bathed in the sea this morning and went for a long walk in the afternoon with Mrs H. After dinner she tried some new songs by

Tchaikovsky. We did not care for them much and fell back on Schubert. Schubert is her favourite composer. She sang the *Gruppe aus Tartarus*.

Wednesday, August 4th.

We went for an expedition to the Lizard. Mrs Housman told me that when she was a girl she had much wanted to become a professional singer, and that she was studying for the Concert Stage when she met Housman.

Thursday, August 5th.

We sat on the beach all the afternoon. It was extremely hot and enjoyable. Mrs Housman read *Consuelo,* by George Sand, aloud. She reads French with great purity of accent.

Father Stanway, the local priest, came to dinner, a cheerful man with a venerable appearance. When we were left alone, after dinner, talking of men in public offices, he said he knew Bowes, in the Foreign Office, who had spent his Easter holidays here. I asked him whether he thought converts of that description made satisfactory Catholics. He said he thought Bowes would be an admirable Catholic. I said I thought it must be very difficult for a man of his upbringing, as Bowes had been brought up in a rigid Church of England family, and his father often wrote to *The Times,* condemning ritualistic practices and innovations. Father Stanway said it was not so complicated as I thought. There were only three things indispensable to a man if he wished to become a Catholic: To believe in God, to follow his conscience, to love his neighbour as himself. If he did that all the rest was easy. He said he admired Bowes greatly for taking the step.

Friday, August 6th.

We went to the Land's End, where there were a great many tourists. Mrs Housman continues to read out loud *Consuelo* in the afternoons and evenings. It is an interesting book, but I prefer *Jane Eyre.*

Saturday, August 7th.

I received a letter from Riley this morning. He has been in London nearly a month, and was there a fortnight before I left, but he did not come to see me for the following reason. He has taken the step and has been received into the Roman Catholic Church, and he says his first intention was not to tell anyone of his conversion. He did not come to see me because he knew he would not be able to help discussing it. He is no longer making a secret of it now. He found this too difficult. Two or three days after he had been received he happened to be dining out and it was a Friday. His hostess said to him, in the course of conversation:

"You are not a Catholic, are you?" He resolved then and there to keep it secret no longer.

He tells me in his letter, "Your philosophy of the first lie is quite right. Only I regard what you call the first lie as the *first Truth*. Once this is so, all the rest follows." He says that after he left me in Gray's Inn in May he resolved to put the matter from him for a time and not to think about it. He went back to Paris and pursued his research. One morning he woke up and felt he could not delay another moment. He took the train for London the next day, where he intended to go soon in any case for his holiday, and the day after his arrival he called at the Brompton Oratory and asked to see a priest, as he knew no priests. He sat in a small waiting-room downstairs, and presently an elderly priest, Father X., arrived and asked him what he could do for him. He told him he wished for instruction prior to becoming a Catholic. He called the next day. Father X. told him after they had talked for some time that he did not think he would need much instruction. But he continued to see him for the next three weeks. He was then received. He says that what seemed before a step of great difficulty now appeared quite extraordinarily simple, and he cannot conceive why he did not take it a long time ago.

Sunday, August 8th.

Mrs Housman went to Mass. I sat in the garden; when she returned from Mass I told her about Riley. She asked me how old he was. I said I thought he was about thirty-five. I told her he was a brilliant scholar, and had taken high honours at Oxford. He had a post at the Liverpool University. She said she had felt certain he would come into the Church.

Lady Jarvis is coming here next week.

Monday, August 9th.

We spent the whole day on the beach, reading aloud. Housman has written to say that Mrs Carrington-Smith will insist on bringing their affairs into court. Carrington-Smith is much worried. Mrs Housman says that Mrs Carrington-Smith is an absurd woman.

Tuesday, August 10th.

We spent the morning at St Ives, shopping. I bought *The Pickwick Papers* and an old silver teapot. We sat on the beach in the afternoon, reading *Consuelo.* After dinner Mrs Housman sang a beautiful French-Canadian song.

Wednesday, August 11th.

Just as we were sitting down to luncheon A. walked into the room; he had sailed here from Cowes in his yacht, which is anchored in the bay. He could not stay to luncheon as he was lunching at the Golf Club with a friend. Mrs Housman asked him to dinner. He accepted. He said he had spent a most enjoyable week at Cowes in his yacht, but had not won any races. His sister had been with him, only as she is a bad sailor she had not enjoyed the sailing as much as he would have liked. Cunninghame has been at Cowes for three days on board a Mr Venderling's steam yacht (an American). A. says that he intends to spend some time here cruising about the coast.

Thursday, August 12th.

Lady Jarvis arrived this morning. She says she thinks that if Mrs Carrington-Smith goes into court she will get a divorce. She has substantial evidence. Carrington-Smith is most uneasy.

A. came to luncheon and proposed that we should all go for a sail in the afternoon together. Lady Jarvis and I declined, as we are both moderate sailors. Mrs Housman went with him. They came back at six and she said she had enjoyed it immensely.

Friday, August 13th.

Mrs Housman received a telegram from Housman this morning, telling her she must ask A. to stay here in the house. She had written to tell him—Housman—A. was here. A. came to luncheon and Mrs Housman invited him to stay. He said he would be pleased to do so for a few days, but that he is due in his yacht early next week at Plymouth. Mrs Housman has received a letter from Cunninghame, asking whether it would be convenient for him to come next week. She has telegraphed to him that she would be glad to receive him.

Saturday, August 14th.

The weather was so beautiful and the sea was so smooth that we were all persuaded to go on board the yacht, where we had luncheon. We went for a short sail in the afternoon. Although I did not feel ill I cannot say I enjoyed it, I prefer the dry land. Lady Jarvis said she enjoyed it greatly, although she is a bad sailor as a rule. Mrs Housman is an excellent sailor.

Sunday, August 15th.

I am finishing *Consuelo* by myself as we are not able to read aloud any more. We all went for a drive in two carriages in the afternoon through disused mines, and had tea in a farm-house.

A. says he is enjoying his holiday immensely.

Cunninghame arrives here to-morrow. We had some music in the evening. A.'s favourite composer is Sullivan, but his favourite song is Offenbach's *Chanson de Fortunio*, which Mrs Housman sang to-night.

Letters from Guy Cunninghame to Mrs Caryl

GREY FARM,
CARBIS BAY, CORNWALL,
Tuesday, August 17th.
DEAREST ELSIE,

I arrived here from Worsel last night, and found Mrs Housman, Lady Jarvis, George, who sailed here in his yacht from Cowes, and Godfrey Mellor. It is the most delicious place. A blue sea with pink and purple streaks in it, and a soft west wind, and wonderful sand beaches, thick with people. It is the height of the season. The Housmans have got a comfortable little house near a golf links. Housman has had to go to London to see his partner, Carrington-Smith, who has been threatened with divorce by his wife, who accuses him of infidelity with—who do you think?—Eileen Hope. "Bert" is by way of coming down here on Saturday. George is radiantly happy. I don't think she's thinking about him. He wanted us all to go out in his yacht this afternoon, but as it was blowing half a gale Mrs Housman was the only one who faced the elements. She is a passionately good sailor and the rougher it is the more she enjoys it. I played golf with a General York who lives here. Godfrey Mellor doesn't play, which is tiresome. We are having the greatest fun. Lady Jarvis is in the most splendid form. She told us some killing stories about Mrs Carrington-Smith. She says that the whole of last year she would only eat raw roots and uncooked fruit because she says in a former existence she was a priestess of I sis, and that was the rule. Lady Jarvis pointed out to her that she is not a priestess of I sis now, but she said that if she ate meat it would spoil her chance of serving Isis again in her next existence. She said, too, that it would displease the elementals. Mrs Housman seems perfectly happy and cheerful. Mellor is depressed, but I am terribly sorry for him. I feel he was having such a divine time here before we all came.

GREY FARM,
Monday, August 23rd.
DEAREST ELSIE,

"Bert" came down on Saturday night, but went away this morning. He is completely upset about Carrington-Smith, who says his wife is bent on divorcing him. Now that he is gone one can laugh, but while he was there we simply didn't dare. Eileen was apparently a most imprudent correspondent. Housman says she will win her case without any doubt if she brings it into court. I played golf with him all Sunday.

We had great fun after dinner last night. Mrs Housman sang songs out of the Gilbert and Sullivan operas, and some Offenbach, too, the

Chanson de Fortunio, too beautifully. George *is* desperately in love—but I still don't think *she* is.

Yours,

G.

GREY FARM, CARBIS BAY,

Tuesday, August 24*th.*

DEAREST ELSIE,

I am going to stay another week as Edith can't have me yet. George was leaving to-day, as he has got to be at Plymouth for a regatta somewhere, but he has put off going till to-morrow because of the weather.

I am enjoying myself immensely. I have got to like Godfrey Mellor very much. I went for a long walk with him one afternoon. When one gets him quite alone like that he talks quite a lot and is delightful.

Mrs Carrington-Smith *is* going to insist on divorce.

I am going to the Shamiers' on the 1st of October. I told you they have been lent a lodge in Scotland on the coast.

Yours etc.,

G.

From the Diary of Godfrey Mellor

Monday, August 16*th. Grey Farm, Carbis Bay.*

Cunninghame arrived late in the evening. We talked at dinner a great deal about the likelihood of the Carrington-Smith divorce. We discussed divorce in general. Mrs Housman was of course against divorce, but she said that the rules of the Church were terribly hard on the individual in many cases. She said: "We are allowed to separate."

Tuesday, August 17*th.*

We all went for an expedition to the Land's End.

Wednesday, August 18*th.*

We all bathed in the morning. Mrs Carrington-Smith has refused to relent in spite of Housman's attempts at mediation—apparently she found some letters addressed by Miss Hope to her husband and Miss Hope was an imprudent correspondent. Lady Jarvis and I wondered why people kept letters, especially when they were compromising. Mrs Housman said she quite understood this. She never could bring herself to burn old letters, although she never looked at them.

Thursday, August 19*th.*

We had luncheon on board the yacht, but after luncheon we left A. on board and went for a walk on the cliffs.

Friday, August 20*th.*

I went for a walk with Cunninghame in the afternoon. He talked a great deal about A. He said he ought to marry. He said he thought Mrs Housman was one of the nicest people he had ever met in his life.

Saturday, August 21st.

Housman arrived in the evening. It poured with rain all day, so we sat indoors. Lady Jarvis played patience. Mrs Housman played some old songs she found in the house. There is nothing, I think, more melancholy than old or, rather, old-fashioned music.

Sunday, August 22nd.

Housman announced his intention of going to Mass with Mrs Housman this morning. He said he always did so at the seaside, he thought it right to support poor Missions. Housman said at luncheon that Father Stanway had preached an excellent sermon. He had said in his sermon that man was a ridiculous animal, and that every time we slip on a piece of orange-peel or sit down on a hat by mistake, we should give thanks for the Grace of God that is teaching us humility. In the afternoon Cunninghame and Housman played golf. Housman lost. He says Cunninghame is a very fine player.

Monday, August 23rd.

Housman left for London this morning. A. leaves to-morrow for Plymouth, but the weather is still very unsettled and it has been blowing hard, and I wonder whether he will be able to start.

Last night after dinner Mrs Housman suggested reading aloud. A. asked her to read some stories by an American called O. Henry, whose works have not been published in England, and whom I had never heard of. A. has travelled in America. Mrs Housman did so. She said she thought we would find them difficult to understand as we did not know America. We did, that is to say, Cunninghame and myself. But A. was greatly amused, and Lady Jarvis said she thought they were clever.

Tuesday, August 24th.

It is still blowing hard and A. has put off going to Plymouth altogether, as he would not get there in time for the regatta. Cunninghame and A. played golf to-day with a retired Indian General, who lives in a house about three miles from here. His name is York. They brought him back to tea, a brisk, direct man. He said something about his wife and Mrs Housman asked if she might call on her. General York said they would be delighted.

More O. Henry was read out in the evening. I prefer Mrs Housman's readings in French literature. A. enjoyed it immensely.

Wednesday, August 25th.

Mrs Housman called on Mrs York this afternoon. Mrs York greeted her with the words: "This is very unusual." Mrs Housman did not understand what was unusual. Mrs York said she did not recollect having called. She was the oldest inhabitant and had discovered the place. Mrs Housman apologised. She has asked the General and Mrs York to luncheon on Sunday.

Thursday, August 26th.

Cunninghame played golf with the General. I went for a walk with Lady Jarvis in the afternoon. She talked of a great many things; of music and musical education abroad. She considers Mrs Housman a fine artist. She talked of A., of his work and mine and my prospects for the future. I told her I enjoyed routine work and had no ambition to do anything else. She talked of marriage. She said A. ought certainly to marry soon as he would be very lonely otherwise. His sister, Mrs Campion, could not look after him, as she had her own children to look after. Her eldest daughter would soon be out. She asked me whether I had ever thought of marrying. She is a most intelligent and agreeable woman.

Friday, August 27th.

A. was obliged to go to Penzance to-day for the day. We all went for a walk in the afternoon. It is finer and quite warm, but the sea is still very rough. Mrs Housman received a letter from Mrs York this morning saying that she was unable to come to luncheon on Sunday, but that she had no doubt the General would accept the invitation with pleasure. Mrs Housman wrote back to say she would be delighted to see the General on Sunday.

The O. Henry book is finished. Mrs Housman is now reading us some stories by another American author, Richard Harding Davis. I wish she would return to European literature. But A. enjoys these American books.

Saturday, August 28th.

The wind has gone down and A. went out sailing. Cunninghame played golf. Mrs Housman spent the day at a convent which is some miles off, and she did not come down to dinner.

Lady Jarvis took me into the town in the morning, and in the afternoon we went for a drive. We had no reading in the evening.

Sunday, August 29th.

General York did not come to luncheon after all, he wrote a note excusing himself. Mrs Housman went to Mass in the morning. A. and Cunninghame played golf. Mrs Housman read out loud a story by Kipling after dinner. I wonder what an E.P. tent means.

Letter from Guy Cunninghame to Mrs Caryl

GREY FARM, CARBIS BAY,

August 30*th.*

DEAREST ELSIE,

The weather has been too awful, but now, thank heaven, it is fine again. George was obliged to put off going to Plymouth by sea as it was too rough. The Shamiers have put me off. They can't have the Lodge that was going to be lent to them, so they won't go to Scotland at all this year. This changes all my plans. Mrs Housman asked me to stay on another week here, and I am going to as there is now no hurry to get to Edith's. I shall then go back to Worsel for three days if they can have me, and then stay with Edith for the rest of my holiday. She has got the whole family there at this moment, so I shall enjoy going there later better. I shall be back in London the first week in October.

There is a charming old man here who plays golf with me, General York. His wife, who was huffy because Mrs Housman "called," paid a call in state this afternoon. She came in a barouche with an Indian servant on the box. She is organising a bazaar and asked Lady Jarvis to help at her stall. She said the bazaar was in the cause of the Church; she did not ask Mrs Housman. She stayed seven minutes by the clock and refused tea, which she said she never took as it was trying for the nerves. She was dressed in black jet, and brought with her a small Pomeranian dog. She said she and her husband had lived here eight years and that it used to be a charming place when they discovered it.

Write to me here and then to Edith's, but not to Worsel as that is uncertain.

Yours,

G.

From the Diary of Godfrey Mellor

Monday, August 30*th.*

I am glad to say Cunninghame has put off going for a week. Mrs York called chis afternoon. I was introduced to her, but she addressed no remark to me.

Tuesday, August 31*st.*

A. has gone away for a night as he is staying with someone in the neighbourhood. Mrs Housman took Cunninghame to the Lizard, which he had not yet seen. Lady Jarvis and I spent a lazy day in the garden and on the cliffs. It is extremely hot.

Wednesday, September 1*st.*

Cunninghame and A. played golf with General York and suggested his coming back to tea, but he declined with much embarrassment. Mrs Housman returned Mrs York's visit, but she was not at home. Mrs Housman sang after dinner. A. does not care for German music, which limits the programme; he is fond, however, of old English songs.

Thursday, September 2nd.

A beautiful day for sailing, so they said. A. took Mrs Housman for a sail.

Friday, September 3rd.

I find A.'s spirits a little boisterous at times. He took us out fishing this afternoon. After dinner he insisted on Mrs Housman playing some American coon songs.

Saturday, September 4th.

Housman arrived unexpectedly with Carrington-Smith this afternoon. Carrington-Smith seems depressed about his coming divorce. Mrs Housman was out sailing with A. and they did not come back until just before dinner. Carrington-Smith is a great expert on boxing and gave us a sparring exhibition after dinner. That is to say, he explained at great length the nature of a straight left, and upset some of the furniture in so doing. After dinner Housman, Carrington-Smith, Cunninghame and Lady Jarvis played Bridge.

Sunday, September 5th.

Housman played golf and met General York, knowing nothing of what had occurred, and asked him and Mrs York to luncheon. The General was much embarrassed and said his wife was an invalid. Housman then asked him to come by himself. The General stammered and said they were having luncheon out. But Housman would take no refusal and asked them to dinner. The General said they didn't dine out on Sundays! His wife——And then he got dreadfully confused, and Cunninghame came to the rescue and said Housman had forgotten we were dining on board the yacht, which we were of course not doing.

Cunninghame leaves, I regret to say, to-morrow.

Letter from Guy Cunninghame to Mrs Caryl

GREY FARM, CARBIS BAY,

Sunday, September 5th.

DEAREST ELSIE,

I leave to-morrow for Worsel. I am only stopping here a week. Then I go on to Edith's where I shall stay to the end of the month. Most of the family have gone. I spent a whole day with Mrs Housman on Tuesday and we went to the Lizard. This is the first time I have had a real talk alone with her since I have been here. We were talking about my plans and I said that I had been going to stay with the Shamiers. She said: "Oh yes," and paused a moment and then said: "She's a charming woman, isn't she?" I could see she knew. Later on she talked of George and said how nice Mrs Campion was and what a good thing it would be if George married. I said: "Yes, what a good thing. It was the greatest mistake his not marrying." Upon which she said: "Do you think he will?" And then in a flash I knew that Lady Jarvis had been quite right and I had been utterly wrong. What an idiot I have been! It must have been quite obvious to a baby the whole time! I can't tell you how I mind it. I think it is the greatest pity and really too awful! What are we to do? That's just it—one can do nothing: there is nothing to be done, absolutely nothing. Of course Godfrey Mellor must have seen it clearly the whole time. I am sure he is miserable. It is all the greatest pity and how I can have been so blind, I don't know, not that it would have made any difference if I hadn't been. Housman, of course, sees nothing and has begged George to stay on. As a matter of fact he (George) is going away quite soon as he has to sail his yacht back and he is stopping somewhere on the way. He will be back in London in October. It is all very depressing and I am quite glad to be going. Lady Jarvis has said nothing to me but I can see that she sees that I see. Godfrey Mellor is staying on. Housman leaves to-morrow. Write to me at Edith's.

Yrs.

G.

From the Diary of Godfrey Mellor

Monday, September 6th.

Housman and Cunninghame both left this morning. A. goes away on Wednesday. A stormy day—too rough for sailing. Carrington-Smith, who is remaining on, played golf with A.

Tuesday, September 7th.

Mrs Housman and A. went out for a sail. I went for a walk with Lady Jarvis. Carrington-Smith played golf: after dinner he sang *I'll sing thee songs of Araby,* Mrs Housman accompanied him: he has a tenor voice.

Wednesday, September 8th.

A. left in his yacht this morning. Lady Jarvis took Carrington-Smith for a walk. I went out with Mrs Housman. She suggested finishing *Consuelo*: I told her I had already finished it. Miss Housman arrives on Saturday.

Thursday, September 9th.

Mrs Housman received a telegram from Mrs Baines, who is in the neighbourhood with her husband, proposing themselves. Mrs Housman has asked them to stay. They will arrive to-morrow. Carrington-Smith sang Tosti's *Good-bye* after dinner.

I went for a walk with Mrs Housman in the afternoon. She said she likes Cunninghame particularly. She said that A. ought to marry.

Friday, September 10*th.*

A rainy day, we remained indoors. Carrington-Smith went for a walk by himself. Mr and Mrs Baines arrived in the afternoon. After dinner they played bridge: Lady Jarvis, Carrington-Smith and Mr and Mrs Baines. Mrs Baines said she greatly admired the works of Mrs Ella Wheeler Wilcox. "She is," she said, "a true poet, or perhaps I should say a true poetess." She said theatrical performances affected her so much that she could seldom "sit out a piece." She had been obliged to take to her bed after seeing *The Only Way*. Carrington-Smith said he preferred a prize fight to any play. Mr Baines did not care for the English stage, but he always went to a French play when there was one to see in London: he had greatly admired Sarah Bernhardt in old days. His wife, he pensively reminded us, had once been taken for her. Mrs Baines protested and said that it was in the days when Sarah Bernhardt was quite thin. "Such a beautiful voice," she said. "Quite the human violin in those days. Now, of course, she rants and appears in such dreadful plays—so violent."

Saturday, September 11*th.*

Mr and Mrs Baines left this morning. Miss Housman arrived in the afternoon. Carrington-Smith played golf and I went out with Mrs Housman. After dinner Miss Housman suggested Bridge, but there were only three players, as Mrs Housman does not play. Miss Housman said I must play. I said I did not know the rules. She said she would teach me. I played—I was her partner. She became excited over what is called the "double ruff," a point I have not yet grasped. Carrington-Smith, who is an excellent player, explained me the rules with great patience.

Sunday, September 12*th.*

Mrs Housman went to Mass. In the afternoon she went for a walk with Miss Housman. We played Bridge again after dinner. Miss Housman was annoyed with me as I neglected to finesse.

Monday, September 13*th.*

The last week of my holiday. It becomes finer and warmer every day. Miss Housman said she must see the Land's End. Mrs Housman took her there. I went for a walk with Lady Jarvis in the evening. More

Bridge after dinner: I revoked, but my partner, Carrington-Smith, was most amiable about it.

Tuesday, September 14th.

Miss Housman took Mrs Housman into the town as she said she needed help with her shopping: she did not make many purchases. As far as I understood, only two yards of silk. I went out with Carrington-Smith in the afternoon. Bridge in the evening—I do not yet understand the "double ruff."

Wednesday, September 15th.

We all went to the Lizard in two carriages. Miss Housman said she must see the Lizard. She, Mrs Housman and myself went in one carriage; Lady Jarvis and Carrington-Smith in the other. Bridge in the evening; Miss Housman lost, which annoyed her.

Thursday, September 16th.

A wet day. Miss Housman practised all the morning (Fantasia in C sharp minor, Chopin); her touch is very metallic. We played Bridge in the afternoon after tea, as well as after dinner.

Friday, September 17th.

My last day. It cleared up. We all went out on to the beach. Miss Housman read aloud a novel, which she had already begun and which we will certainly not have time to finish, called *Queed,* by an American author. After dinner we played Bridge.

Saturday, September 18th.

Arrived at Gray's Inn. Travelled up with Carrington-Smith.

Sunday, October 3rd. Gray's Inn.

Stayed at home in the morning and read the Sunday newspapers. In the afternoon I went for a walk in Kensington Gardens.

Monday, October 4th.

A. and Cunninghame returned to the office. A. told us that his sister, Mrs Campion, had invited both of us to stay with her next Saturday at her house in Oxfordshire. We have both accepted.

Tuesday, October 5th.

Cunninghame asked me to dinner. We dined at his flat and sat up talking until nearly one o'clock in the morning. I had a letter from Lady Jarvis telling me she has returned to London and inviting me to visit her in Mansfield Street whenever I felt inclined.

Wednesday, October 6th.

Dined with A. at his Club. He told me that Mrs Housman arrives to-morrow; he met Housman in the street this morning.

Thursday, October 7th.

I called on Lady Jarvis late this evening and found her at home. She said Cornwall had had a beneficial effect on Mrs Housman's health. I stayed talking till nearly seven.

Friday, October 8th.

Received a note from Mrs Housman asking me to dine there next Tuesday. Went to a concert with Lady Jarvis at the Queen's Hall: the programme was uninteresting, but I enjoyed my evening nevertheless.

Saturday, October 9th. Wraxted Priory, Oxfordshire.

I travelled down with A. and Cunninghame and found a party consisting, besides ourselves, of Mrs Campion and her three children, Fräulein Brandes, the governess, Miss Macdonald, Cunninghame's cousin, and a Miss Wray. I sat next to Mrs Campion at dinner: she said she hoped they would go to Florence again next Easter. After dinner we played Consequences and the letter game.

Sunday, October 10th.

Everyone went to church this morning except Cunninghame and myself. At luncheon I sat next to Fräulein Brandes. She said Shakespeare was badly performed in England and that she preferred the German translation of the plays to the original; she considered it superior. "*Aber das*," she added, "*will kein Engländer gestehen*." She was shocked to hear I had never read Shakespeare's plays. I told her I had no taste for verse. She said this was *unglaublich*. I told her I was fond of German music. In the afternoon Mrs Campion took me for a walk. Cunninghame went out with his cousin. At dinner I sat next to Miss Wray. I found her most agreeable. She has travelled a great deal and seems to have a real appreciation of classical music.

Letter from Guy Cunninghame to Mrs Caryl

LONDON,

Monday, October 11th.

DEAREST ELSIE,

We had a delightful Sunday at Mrs Campion's. A lovely old house not very far from Oxford: grey stone walls, a hall with the walls left bare and a few bits of good tapestry and another panelled room. Freda was there, and Lavinia Wray, who has just come back from South America. She is looking so well, her lovely skin whiter than ever and those huge eyes—George liked her enormously. He had never met her before. How wonderful it would be if that could come off. It would be exactly right. Of course I am sure Mrs Campion wants it and is not likely to do anything stupid. I shall get Edith to help later if possible. She is still in the country now. Mrs Housman has come back to London and I hear from Randall that Housman is mad about Mrs Park. I shall go and see her next week. George is in good spirits. When I got back I couldn't bear the sight of my flat with those glaring curtains and I have committed the great extravagance of changing them. The new ones are coming next week. I hope they will be a success as I shan't be able to change them again.

Yrs.

G.

From the Diary of Godfrey Mellor

Monday, October 11*th.*

Dined at the Club.

Tuesday, October 12*th.*

Had luncheon with Cunninghame to meet his sister, Mrs Howard. She is older than he is and less communicative. Her husband is on the Stock Exchange. She was only in London for the day but she said she hoped I would come and see her when she settled in London later. She has a house in Chester Street.

Wednesday, October 13*th.*

Dined with the Housmans last night. A. was there, Miss Housman and Mrs Park. I sat next to Mrs Housman. Mrs Park contradicted A. when he mentioned music and said something about the gross ignorance of English amateurs. After dinner she asked Miss Housman to accompany her. She sang some operatic airs and Gounod's *Ave Maria.* I drove home with A., who told me he could not bear Mrs Park.

Thursday, October 14*th.*

I am just back from dining with Lady Jarvis. A. was there, Miss Wray and several other people. Lady Jarvis asked me if I had seen the Housmans. I told her about my dinner there. She said that Mrs Park was an intolerable woman: she knew her when she was a singer and she said she had never met anyone who gave herself such airs. Walked home with Cunninghame, who was dining there too. He is dining with the Housmans on Sunday. The Carrington-Smith divorce case is in the newspapers.

Friday, October 15*th.*

Dined at the Club.

Mrs Carrington-Smith has got her divorce.

Saturday, October 16*th.*

Spent the day at Woking with Solway. He has finished his Sonata.

Sunday, October 17*th.*

I went to see Mrs Housman this afternoon and found her at home. After I had been there about five minutes a great many visitors arrived and I left.

Letter from Guy Cunninghame to Mrs Caryl

HALKIN STREET,

Sunday, October 17*th.*

DEAREST ELSIE,

I am having a quiet Sunday in London. George is staying with the Prime Minister. I dined last night with the Housmans. Mrs Park was there, Randall and Miss Housman. Mrs Park is incredible: a magnificent figure, hair dyed a rich bronze with flaming high lights, dressed in a flowing robe of peach-coloured satin with a necklace of fire-opals and a large diamond lyre on her shoulder; the semi-royal manner of an ex-Prima Donna, at the same time making it quite clear that she no longer mixed with the artistic world—she had soared to the top of it and out of it. She said: "Years ago when I was at Balmoral the dear Queen told me she reminded me of Grisi." I said: "I suppose you mean you reminded her of Grisi," and she drew herself up stiffly and said she meant what she said. She told me that Madame Cosima had implored her to sing at Bayreuth but of course she couldn't think of doing such a thing. Poor Theodore (her late husband) hated Wagner. After dinner she sang, Miss Housman accompanied her, a song out of *Cavalleria.* They had a fierce argument about the time. Mrs Park said she was playing too fast, which she was, although I don't believe Mrs Park knew this. Miss Sarah stuck to her guns and played, if anything, faster. Mrs Park then refused to sing. Housman asked his wife to accompany her, which Mrs Housman most good-naturedly said she would be delighted to do. This was more than Miss Housman could bear—she said Mrs Housman was playing too slow and Mrs Park agreed. Miss Housman tore Mrs Housman from the piano and sat there herself, and the song was sung to the end. All seemed to be peaceable but Miss Housman unfortunately couldn't refrain from saying that Mascagni's music was rubbish, upon which Mrs Park burst into a furious passion. Who was Miss Housman to judge? she screamed. Miss Housman said she had studied music for five years under the best musicians in the world at Leipzig. Mrs Park said she had sung to Patti, who had said she was the only English artist worthy of the name of "artist." Miss Housman, in a sardonic voice, said that Patti was so kind. Mrs Park said that the arrogance of amateurs knew no bounds. She had sung before the most critical public in two continents. Miss Housman said she did not consider the Americans a critical public. Mrs

Park then said she would never sing again in the Housmans' house as long as she lived, not if everyone went down on their knees to her. Housman became greatly agitated and fussed about the room, saying: "Never mind, never mind; we are all very tired to-night, it's the east wind." Mrs Park said she always sang her best in an east wind. I caught Mrs Housman's eye and we were seized with a fit of uncontrollable laughter. We laughed till we shook. Randall caught it too. This made things much worse. Mrs Park said she was being insulted and swept out of the room, Housman running after her. He came back alone gibbering with agitation, and Miss Housman then attacked him and said of course if Albert (rolling the "r" with a rapid guttural) would invite such awful people, what could one expect? Then "Bert" got really angry and we all sat in dead silence while he and Miss Sarah abused each other like pickpockets. Then the door opened and Mrs Park came back saying she had left her fan behind. She took no notice of us but disappeared with Housman into the Oriental lounge, and there we heard spirited skirmishes of talk going on in an undertone. Miss Housman sat down defiantly at the piano and played, or rather banged, the *Rapsodie Hongroise.* When this was over they both came back and Housman suggested, with a nervous chuckle, that we should all have some lemonade. We jumped at the idea and the evening ended peaceably enough, but Mrs Park ignored Miss Housman, was icy towards Mrs Housman, and made all her remarks to me and Randall. I then left the house. Housman followed me nervously to the door and said that Mrs Park had the artistic temperament and that I mustn't mind, and that it was too bad of Sarah to provoke her.

Yrs.

G.

P.S.—I suppose you read about the Carrington-Smith case in the newspapers. Mrs Housman and I laughed a good deal about it when "Bert" wasn't listening, but I am very sorry for Eileen. Aren't you?

From the Diary of Godfrey Mellor

Monday, October 18*th.*

A. has been staying with the Prime Minister. He does not appear to have enjoyed himself very much. He asked me if I had seen the Housmans lately.

Tuesday, October 19*th.*

A. and I dined with Cunninghame. Miss Wray was there, Mrs Howard and Lady Jarvis. A. said afterwards that Miss Wray was a charming girl—it was a pity that she did not marry.

Wednesday, October 20th.

I called on Mrs Housman late, but she was not at home. Housman came out of the house as I was standing at the door. He asked me to dinner on Sunday. I accepted.

Thursday, October 21st.

Dined at the Club.

Friday, October 22nd.

Dined with Mrs Howard. A. was there, Cunninghame, Miss Wray, Miss Macdonald, and others. Mr Howard is half-Irish and very boisterous. I sat next to Miss Wray; she said Mrs Campion was the nicest woman she knew. Uncle Arthur and Aunt Ruth have come back to London and are starting their Thursday evenings. They have asked A. and myself to dinner on Thursday week.

Saturday, October 23rd.

A. has gone to the country to stay with a General; a military party.

Sunday, October 24th.

I had luncheon with Lady Jarvis. She told me she did not think Mrs Housman would stay long in London, as the London winter was bad for her; she said she thought she would most likely go to Florence.

I dined with the Housmans. A strange party. Mrs Park was the only person there I had met before. There was a South African magnate and his wife, a retired Indian official, and a Mr Perry, an Australian, and his wife, who were apparently intimate friends of Mrs Park's, at least she called him Tom. I sat next to Mrs Perry, who told me that Paris had been a disappointment to her. She told me, also, that the women in England were, according to Australian standards, dowdy. On the other side of me was Lady Bowles, the wife of the Indian official. She told me she was Mrs Park's greatest friend; she said she lived at Cannes and only spent a few weeks in London every year; they were staying at the Hyde Park Hotel. She found London dreadfully slow: she was accustomed, she said, always to smoke between the courses at dinner, and not to do so was a great deprivation. She also said she was a great gambler and was used to gambling all night. "Of course I find this exhausting," she said; "and I always tell Harold I shall take to cocaine some day." Housman seemed rather embarrassed. Miss Housman was not there. After dinner Lady Bowles suggested a game of Poker. They all played except Mrs Housman and they were still playing when I left.

Monday, October 25th.

I had luncheon with Cunninghame at his Club. He said A. had come back from the country in a very bad temper and had said that nothing would induce him to pay a visit anywhere again.

Tuesday, October 26th.

Went to a concert at the Queen's Hall. Saw the Housmans in the distance, and to my astonishment I met A. in the interval. He said he had been dragged there by his sister. I met them again as we were going out. A. asked me to dinner on Friday.

Wednesday, October 27th.

Had luncheon with A. He seems in high spirits. He told me that his sister had come up from London for the winter—she had taken a house in Pont Street. He said the Housmans and Cunninghame were dining on Friday and it would be a Cornwall party.

Thursday, October 28th.

Dined with Aunt Ruth—a large political dinner; the F.O. largely represented, as usual. A. was there and sat next to the wife of the French military attache, and on the other side of Aunt Ruth. I am afraid he found the dinner tedious, but after dinner he talked to Miss Wray: I sat next to her at dinner. She asked me if I had known A. long. She said he was so like his sister. Uncle Arthur has not yet grasped I am working in a public office. He asked me how I was getting on in the city.

Friday, October 29th.

Dined with A. at his flat. Mr and Mrs Housman, Lady Jarvis, Miss Wray, Cunninghame and Miss Macdonald, Mrs Campion was coming but had been obliged to go down to the country. Mrs Housman said she was very likely going abroad for the winter.

Saturday, October 30th.

A. was engaged to go somewhere in the country but he has put off going. He left a telegram at the office to his hostess but forgot to fill in the address. Tuke brought it to me. It was to Mrs Legget, Miss Wray's aunt. She is not in *Who's Who*, but I rang up Lady Jarvis on the telephone and she knew.

Sunday, October 31st.

I went to call on Mrs Housman but she was not at home.

Letter from Guy Cunninghame to Mrs Caryl

LONDON,

Monday, November 1st.

DEAREST ELSIE,

I spent Sunday in London and had luncheon with Lady Jarvis. She told me the Housman *ménage* was all upside down owing to Mrs Park, who refused to let Housman see any of his old friends, insulted them all, and quarrelled every day with Miss Housman, and insisted on her friends being asked nightly to dinner—and what friends! Fast colonials, Lady Jarvis says, and the dregs of the Riviera! Poor Mrs Housman is utterly worn out. Mrs Park behaves exactly as if it were her house, orders the servants about, complains of the food, and is always there! The result is Mrs Housman has gone to Florence; she was to leave this morning and she is going to stay there the whole winter. I did not know how George would take this bit of news, but he knew already and seems, oddly enough, in good spirits! Edith thinks he is fond of Lavinia Wray and that he will end by marrying her, but Lady Jarvis does not agree, although she said that his sister thinks the same thing. They can't understand his being in such spirits otherwise. Last Friday we all had dinner at George's flat. After dinner, so Lady Jarvis told me, before we came out of the dining-room they were playing the game of saying who you could marry and who you couldn't, and after mentioning a lot of people, Godfrey Mellor among others, Freda Macdonald said: "George." Lady Jarvis and Freda said: "Oh yes; we could marry him." Mrs Housman and Lavinia Wray said: "No—quite impossible."

Except Lady Jarvis, they are all extraordinarily optimistic about George and think that there is nothing in the Housman thing and that it will pass off and he will marry Lavinia. I am sure they are wrong, and I am more depressed about it than words can say. Lavinia is fond of him, too, and that is all that has been gained. There are now three miserable people, instead of two! No letter from you this week, but I hope to get one to-morrow.

Yrs.

G.

From the Diary of Godfrey Mellor

Monday, November 1st. Gray's Inn.

Received a letter from Mrs Housman saying that she was leaving for Florence this morning, She was sorry not to have seen me yesterday. She is going to stay in Florence until the end of May.

Tuesday, November 2nd.

Had dinner with A. alone at his flat. He was in low spirits and said that he hates official life.

Tuesday, December 21st.

My Christmas holidays begin to-morrow. I am going to Aunt Ruth's. Cunninghame is staying with Lady Jarvis. A. said he would most probably spend Christmas with his sister, but he was not sure.

Thursday, December 23rd.

Received a telegram from Aunt Ruth saying the party was put off as Uncle Arthur has got bronchitis. A telegram arrived for A. at the office this morning. I telephoned to Tuke at his flat to know where to forward it. Tuke said A.'s address for the next week would be Hotel Grande Bretagne, Florence.

Christmas Day.

Dined at the Club.

Tuesday, December 28th.

Tuke telephoned to say not to forward any more letters to A. He was on his way home.

Saturday, January 8th, 1910.

Received a letter from A. from his sister's house. He is coming up next week. Riley has written to me from Paris to know whether I could put him up next month. He is going to spend a month in London. I have told him I would be glad of his company.

Letters from Guy Cunninghame to Mrs Caryl

ROSEDALE,

Saturday, January 1st, 1910.

DEAREST ELSIE,

I have been staying with Lady Jarvis for Christmas. There is a very small party, only Jane Vaughan and Winchester Hill besides myself. Just before I came down here Housman asked me to dine with him at the Carlton. I went and he was alone. After talking nervously on ordinary topics, he told me he did not know what to do. It gradually came out that Mrs Park is making his life quite unbearable. She won't let him see any of his friends; she quarrels with Sarah, and has the most violent scenes; she makes scenes every day, and not long ago, he said, broke a fine piece of Venetian glass. He is miserable; he says he can't call his soul his own. I told Lady Jarvis all about this and she said the only thing to be done would be for Housman to get Mrs Housman to come back. She has been away two months, and if she comes back at the end of the month the worst of the winter will be over. She is very much worried about Mrs Housman and says this is most unfortunate, as it would be better really in every way if she were to stay out there. You see Edith and Mrs Campion and Freda all think that it is only a passing fancy of George's and that he will get over it and marry Lavinia Wray! Lady Jarvis says this is wrong; she knows they are wrong. She thinks George and Mrs Housman are desperately in love with each other and she doesn't know how it will end. She is so worried that she nearly went out to Florence last week. She had heard from Mrs Housman quite lately. She said in her last letter that George had suggested coming out to Florence for Christmas with Mrs Campion. She had told him that she would most likely not be in Florence as the Albertis had asked her to spend Christmas with them at Ravenna; she was not sure, however, whether she would go or not. Whether George went or not, I don't know. He told me he was going to spend Christmas with Mrs Campion at the Priory.

I am going back to London at the end of next week.

Yrs.

G.

LONDON,

Wednesday, January 11*th.*

DEAREST ELSIE,

I came back to London on Monday. I asked Housman to dinner with me and told him that he had much better get Mrs Housman back. He said he quite agreed that it was the only thing to do. Things were now worse than ever. Mrs Park was impossible. Poor little "Bert"! The worst of it is, that directly this is over there is quite certain to be someone else and perhaps someone worse. However, let us hope for the best. George came to the office yesterday. He said he had been staying with his sister; he said nothing about Florence. He is in low spirits.

I shall certainly go abroad at Easter and spend a few days in Paris in any case. Lady Jarvis is back in London, and the Shamiers. I dined there last night. Lavroff was there and Louise is just as fond of him as ever.

Poor Godfrey Mellor is terribly melancholy. He has got a friend staying with him now and I don't see much of him.

Yrs.

G.

From the Diary of Godfrey Mellor

Tuesday, February 15*th,* 1910.

Alfred Riley arrived last night. He is now professor at Shelborough University and is editing *Propertius*. He has come to consult some books at the British Museum.

Wednesday, February 16*th.*

Sat up very late last night talking with Riley. He was amused by a conversation he had overheard at a Club. Two men were talking about someone who had become a Roman Catholic. Someone he didn't know. One of them said to the other that it was a very pleasant solution if you could do it. The other one said: "Certainly; no bother, no responsibility ... everything settled for you." I said that I did think the Confessional must be the negation of responsibility. Riley said that by becoming a Catholic you became responsible for all your actions. He said that before he was a Catholic he felt no responsibility at all to anything or anyone, but that the moment you were a Catholic everything you did and said counted. Every time you went to Confession you acknowledged and confirmed your assumption of responsibility. I mentioned a common friend of ours, O'Neil, who had been a Catholic all his life and who, though he was married, had never ceased to live with a Miss Silvia Thorpe, whom I had known as an artist. He didn't hide it, neither did she. Riley said that this proved his point. O'Neil never dreamt of going to Confession; he knew it would be useless, because he had no intention of giving up Miss Thorpe, and that being so, he knew he couldn't get Absolution, It was a sacrifice to him, a very great sacrifice, as he Was a believing Catholic. "That shows," he went on, "that you don't understand how the thing works. You and all Protestants think that one can stroll into the Confessional, wipe the slate clean and go on with what you are doing, however bad it is, with the implied sanction of the Church. But the fact remains that practising Catholics who are living in a way which the Church condemned do not go to Confession. Going to Confession entails facing responsibility instead of evading it." He said that if what I thought was true, people like O'Neil would go to Confession. I must face the fact that he did not go to Confession and was extremely unhappy on that account. He would like to go to the Sacraments but he had made this great sacrifice with his eyes open. I said that I had always thought the Church was lax about such matters. He said individuals might be lax. The Church was not responsible for the conduct of individuals, but the rule of the Church was absolutely uncompromising. I said O'Neil might be an extreme case, but supposing a devout Catholic married woman had a great man friend, supposing he was very much in love with her, but she was a virtuous woman, faithful to her husband, she could go on seeing the other man as much as she liked? Would the Church forbid it? Riley said the Church would forbid *sin*. Any priest would tell her that if she thought it might lead to sin, she must cut it out of her life. I said that was quite clear, but he was not telling me what I wanted to know. He said: "What is it that you want to know?" I said I must give it up. I couldn't put it into words. I said Roman Catholics were always so matter-of-fact. They handed one opinions and ideas like chocolates wrapped up in silver paper. He said: "You think that, because you would sooner walk naked in the streets than think things out, or call things by their names.

You like leaving them vague. 'Le vague,' Renan said, 'est pire que le faux.'"

I said, going back to the question of responsibility, that I had often heard Catholics themselves complain of the want of responsibility of Catholics. Riley said that might very well be; they might lack a sense of responsibility, just as they might lack a sense of charity or honesty. "You think," he said, "that the Church is perpetually arranging comfortable compromises. Nothing is further from the truth. Nothing is harder on the individual than certain of the commandments of the Church with regard to marriage: for instance, divorce, and the bearing of children. Some of the Church's views were just as hard on the individual as it was hard on a man, who is going to catch a train to see his dying child, to be delayed by a policeman holding up the traffic, but in order to make traffic possible, you had to have a policeman, and the individual couldn't complain however much he might suffer.

"I know a much harder case than O'Neil's," he said: "a colleague of mine who is married and has been completely neglected by his wife. On the other hand, he has been looked after devotedly for years by another woman, who nursed him when he was ill and saved his life. He wants to become a Catholic, but he knows quite well that the Church will not receive him unless he were to give up this woman, whom he adores, and go back to his wife, who is indifferent to him. What you don't understand," he said, "is that the Church is not an air cushion but a rock."

He said I accused the Church of being lax, but many people that he knew found fault with what they called the *hardness* of the Church. But as a matter of fact they had generally to admit that as far as the human race was concerned the Church in such matters of morals was always right. He cited instances of what the Church was right in condemning. I said that one did not need to be Roman Catholic to know that immorality was bad for the State, and that vice was noxious to the individual. The ordinary laymen reach the same conclusions merely by common-sense.

Riley said there were only two points of view in the world: the Catholic point of view or the non-Catholic point of view. All so-called religions which I could mention, including my layman's common-sense view, were either lopped-off branches of Catholicism or shadows of it, or a blind aspiration towards it, or a misguided parallel of it, as of a train that had gone off the rails, or a travesty of it, sometimes serious, and sometimes grotesque: a distortion. The other point of view was the materialist point of view, which he could perfectly well understand anyone holding. It depends, he said, whether you think human life is casual or divine.

I said I could quite well conceive a philosophy which would be neither materialist nor Catholic. He quoted Dr Johnson about everyone having a right to his opinion, and martyrdom being the test. Catholicism, he said, had survived the test; would my philosophy?

As far as I was concerned I admitted that I held no opinion for which I was ready to go to the stake, except, possibly, that *Jane Eyre* was an interesting book.

Monday, February 21*st.*

I heard from Mrs Housman this morning. She returns to-morrow.

Saturday, February 26*th.*

Called on Mrs Housman, and found her in. Housman was there also. They asked me to dinner next Monday.

Sunday, February 27*th. Rosedale.*

I am staying with Lady Jarvis. There is no one else. Lady Jarvis said she was glad Mrs Housman had returned to London.

Letter from Guy Cunninghame to Mrs Caryl

LONDON,

Tuesday, March 1*st.*

DEAREST ELSIE,

I dined with the Housmans last night. Only myself, Miss Sarah, Lady Jarvis, and Godfrey Mellor. Everything as it used to be. Carrington-Smith came in after dinner. He has not been inside the house for months. I don't know what Mrs Housman did nor how it was done, but it *was* done, and done most successfully and quickly! She only came back a week ago. "Bert" looks quite different and is perfectly radiant.

George, I gather, hasn't seen her. They asked him to dinner last night, but he had an official dinner and couldn't come. He asked me whether I had seen her. He said he had been there several times, but she had always been out. He is still most depressed and goes nowhere unless he is absolutely obliged to. The Housmans have asked me to spend Easter at their villa. Lady Jarvis is going, and Godfrey; and Housman told me he was going to ask George. I am going and I shall stop two or three days in Paris on the way.

Lavinia Wray has gone to the south of France with her aunt. The Shamiers are going to Paris next week. They will tell you all the news, not that there is much.

Yrs.

G.

From the Diary of Godfrey Mellor

Monday, February 28th.

A. told me he had not been to the country after all on Saturday.

Tuesday, March 1st.

Dined with the Housmans, a very agreeable dinner. Mrs Housman played and sang after dinner: Brahms' *Lieder*, and some Grieg.

Wednesday, March 2nd.

A. asked me to luncheon. He told me he had been so sorry not to be able to go to the Housmans' last night. He said he had not seen them yet. He was so busy. He asked me how Mrs Housman was and whether Florence had done her good.

Thursday, March 3rd.

I told Riley I had been reading Renan's *Souvenirs d'enfance et de jeunesse,* and that Renan said in this book that there was nothing in Catholic dogmas which raised in him a contrary opinion; nothing either in the political action or in the spirit of the Church, either in the past or in the present, that led him to doubt; but directly he studied the "Higher Criticism" and German text-books his faith in the Church crumbled. I asked Riley what he thought of this. He said people treated German text-books superstitiously then and they still did so now. If German text-books dealt with Shakespeare people could see at once that they were talking nonsense, and that mountains of erudition were being built on a false base, a base which we knew to be false, because we were English; but when they dealt with things more remote, like the Gospels, people swallowed what they said, and accepted any of their theories as infallible dogma. In twenty years' time, he said, nobody will care two straws for the "Higher Criticism."

Riley is going away to-morrow.

Friday, March 4th.

Mrs Housman has written to ask me to come and see her on Sunday afternoon if I am in London.

Dined with Cunninghame at a restaurant and went to the Palace Music Hall afterwards.

Saturday, March 5th.

A. is much annoyed at having to stay with the Foreign Secretary. Dined at the Club.

Sunday, March 6th.

Spent the afternoon at Mrs Housman's. There was nobody there until Housman came in late just when I was going. Housman said we must all meet at Florence. He said he was going to ask A. "But we never see him now," he added. He asked me what A. was doing. I told him he was staying with the Foreign Secretary. He said, of course he was right to attend to his official and especially to his social duties. He said he would ask him to dinner next week. He asked me to dine on Wednesday. Mrs Housman asked me to go to a concert with her on Tuesday.

Monday, March 7th.

Dined at the Club.

Tuesday, March 8th.

Went to a concert in Chelsea with Mrs Housman, Housman and Miss Housman. Solway played, and an excellent violinist, Miss Bowden; Beethoven Sonata (G Major) and Schubert Quartet (D Minor). We all enjoyed the music and the playing. During the interval we went to see Solway. Housman asked him to dinner to-morrow.

Wednesday, March 9th.

Dined with the Housmans. Lady Jarvis, Mrs Campion, Solway, Cunninghame, Mrs Baines, and A. and Miss Housman were there. I sat between Lady Jarvis and Mrs Campion. After dinner Mrs Housman asked Solway to try a song with her, a new English song by a boy who has just left the College of Music. She sang this and after that she sang all the *Winterreise*. Housman asked A. and Mrs Campion to stay with them in Florence. Mrs Campion cannot get away this Easter. A. accepted the invitation.

Thursday, March 10th.

Went after dinner to Aunt Ruth's. Uncle Arthur is quite restored to health. He asked me whether I had been appointed to Paris, still thinking that I was in the F.O. There were a great many people there. Aunt Ruth spoke severely about A. and said she heard he only went out in the Bohemian world. I said he had stayed with the Foreign Secretary last week.

Friday, March 11th.

Dined with Mrs Campion. A. was there and the Albertis, who are over in England. A. said he was much looking forward to Florence. Easter is early this year.

Saturday, March 12th.

A. has gone to Littlehampton. He has asked the Housmans and Cunninghame. I am going to Woking.

Sunday, March 13th.

Spent the day with Solway, who played Bach. Returned by the late train after dinner.

Letter from Guy Cunninghame to Mrs Caryl

LONDON,

Monday, March 14*th.*

DEAREST ELSIE,

I have just come back from Littlehampton, where I spent Sunday with George and his sister. The Housmans were asked and Housman went, but Mrs Housman was not well. I start on Thursday morning and shall be in Paris Thursday night and stay there till Monday. Let us do something amusing. I should like to go to the play one night. But you have probably seen all the best things hundreds of times. I am going on co Florence on Monday. I don't think George has seen much of Mrs Housman. I dined there last Wednesday. Mrs Housman sang the whole evening so that he did not get any talk with her. Godfrey has been much more cheerful lately and even suggested going to a music-hall one night. Mrs Campion is coming to Florence too.

I'm sorry I've been so bad about writing lately. I seem to have had no time and yet to have done nothing, and there have been a series of rather tiresome episodes at the office.

Au revoir till Thursday,

Yours,

G.

From the Diary of Godfrey Mellor

Monday, March 14*th*

A. came back from the country in a gloomy state of mind. He said it was a great mistake to go to the country in March and that his party had been a failure. He said bachelors should not give parties. He asked me to dine with him, which I did. He says he is leaving on Wednesday but will stop two nights in Paris. Mrs Campion is travelling with him.

Tuesday, March 15*th.*

Mrs Housman rang up on the telephone and told me that a young vocalist was dining with them to-morrow night. She wanted a few people to hear her. Would I come? Solway was coming.

Dined with Cunninghame at his Club. He says he has never seen A. so depressed.

Wednesday, March 16*th.*

Dined with the Housmans. Miss Housman, Solway and Lady Jarvis were there. The vocalist, a Miss Byfield, did not arrive till after dinner. Mrs Housman said Miss Byfield was shy and had refused to dine at the last moment. After dinner she sang some songs from the classical composers. She was extremely nervous. Mrs Housman and Solway say she has promise. Housman said to me confidentially that he was sure there was no money in her. The Housmans leave to-morrow. A. left to-day.

Thursday, March 17th.

Cunninghame left to-day. I had dinner with Lady Jarvis. She asked me to travel with her on Saturday. We are both stopping Sunday night in Paris.

Friday, March 18th.

Lunched and dined at the Club. Packed up my things. Am taking some music with me.

Saturday, March 19th. Paris.

Arrived at the Hôtel Saint Romain. Had a pleasant journey with Lady Jarvis.

Sunday, March 20th.

Lady Jarvis took me to see a French friend of hers, Madame Sainton. It was her day. There was a large crowd of men and women in the drawing-room and the dining-room, where there was tea, Madeira and excellent sandwiches. The French take just as much trouble about preparing a good tea as they do to write or to dress well. I was introduced to a famous composer, who talked to me technically about boxing. I was obliged to confess that I knew nothing of the art. It was a pity, I thought, Carrington-Smith was not there. I was also introduced to a French author, who asked me what was the place of Meredith in modern literature, what *les jeunes* thought about him. I was obliged to confess I had never read one line of Meredith. The French author thought I despised him. He asked me: "Quest qu'on lit en Angleterre maintenant avant de se coucher?" I said that I had no idea what *les jeunes* read but that I personally, for a bedside book, preferred *Jane Eyre*.

The French author said "*Tiens*!" He then asked me what I thought of Bernard Shaw. I had again to confess that I had never seen his plays acted. I told him that when I had time to spare I went to concerts. He said: "Ah! la musique," and I felt he was generalising a whole movement in young England towards music.

In the evening we went to the Opéra Comique and heard *Carmen*, which I greatly enjoyed.

Monday, March 21st. Florence. Villa Fersen.

We arrived at Florence this morning. Cunninghame and A. and Mrs Campion were in the same train. The Housmans had been there some days already.

Tuesday, March 22nd.

Cunninghame, Mrs Housman, A. and Mrs Campion went out together. Lady Jarvis stayed at home. I went later in the morning to the Pitti. In the afternoon they went to Fiesole. Housman went to call on some friends. Lady Jarvis and I went for a walk.

Wednesday, March 23rd.

We were invited to luncheon by a Mr Eugene Lowe, a friend of Lady Jarvis. He has a flat in the town on the Pitti side of the river. The Housmans and Cunninghame and myself went. A. and his sister had luncheon with the Albertis. Mr Lowe's flat had the peculiarity that everything in it had been ingeniously diverted from its original purpose. The only other guest besides ourselves was an ex-diplomatist whom I met last year.

Thursday, March 24th.

Lady Jarvis has gone to Venice, where she is staying with friends until next Monday. While we were sight-seeing this morning we met a lady called Mrs Fairburn, who claimed to be an old friend of Mrs Housman. Mrs Housman told me she had met her in America soon after she married, but that she had never known her well. She asked us all to luncheon on Saturday. Mrs Housman accepted for herself and Housman. Cunninghame and I also accepted. A. and his sister were engaged.

In the afternoon Mrs Housman said she was going to hear a Dominican preach. Cunninghame and I asked if we might accompany her. A. said it was no use his going as he did not understand Italian. He was most eloquent.

Friday (Good Friday), March 25th.

Mrs Housman spent the whole morning in church. I went with Cunninghame for a long walk.

Saturday, March 26th.

We had luncheon with Mrs Fairburn, who has a villa on the Fiesole side. She is a widow and always, she says, lives abroad; so much so, she told us, that she had difficulty in speaking English correctly. She gave us no evidence that she spoke any other language with great correctness. She told me she was overjoyed at meeting Mrs Housman, who was her oldest friend. Housman asked her to dinner to-morrow night.

Sunday (Easter Sunday), March 27th.

I went for a walk by myself. When I got back I found various people at the villa and escaped to my room. Mrs Fairburn came to dinner. When Housman said he had been suffering from a headache she exclaimed: "*Poveretto*!" and said she was feeling-rather "*Moche*" herself. Looking at Mrs Housman, she said to me: "She is *ravissante, che bellezza! E vero?*"

Letter from Guy Cunninghame to Mrs Caryl

VILLA FERSEN, FLORENCE,

Easter Monday, March 28th.

DEAREST ELSIE,

We arrived safely and we are a very happy party. Lady Jarvis has gone to Venice to stay with the Lumleys, but comes back to-morrow. George is, of course, immensely happy at being here, but it isn't really satisfactory. We haven't seen many people, though we have been out to luncheon twice: once with that terrible bore, Eugene Lowe, who lives in a flat which is the most monstrous ind absurd thing I have ever seen. The walls are hung with Turkish carpets; the chairs and tables with Church vestments; the books turn out to be cigarette lamps and cigar cases; the writing-table is a gutted spinet; and in the middle of the room there is a large Venetian well, which he uses for cigarette ashes.

On Saturday we had luncheon with a Mrs Fairburn, who professed to be an old friend of Mrs Housman's. This turned out to be a gross exaggeration. She is an affected woman who dresses in what are meant to be ultra-French clothes, and she speaks broken English on purpose. She pretends to be silly, but is far from being anything of the kind. I can see now that she has got her eye on Housman. He was quite charmed by her. She has arranged an outing next week. I can see that she is going to stick like a leech, and she will be, unless I am very much mistaken, much worse than Mrs Park or any of them.

Godfrey Mellor is, I think, liking it, but he insists on going out by himself, and every day he goes to some gallery with a Baedeker, all alone. We always ask him to come with us, but it is no use. He says he has got things to do in the town and off he goes.

We go about mostly all together except for Godfrey, who always manages to elude us.

I am staying till Monday, then two days at Mentone, and then home (via Paris, but only for a night).

Yrs.

G.

From the Diary of Godfrey Mellor

Monday (Easter Monday), March 28th.

We all had luncheon with the Albertis. Lady Jarvis returned in the afternoon from Venice.

Tuesday, March 29th.

Went to the Uffizzi. Housman said he was going to spend the day in visits.

Wednesday, March 30th.

Mrs Fairburn came to luncheon. Housman said when she had gone that she was a very remarkable woman, so cultivated, so well read and widely travelled. He said she ought to have held some great position. She should have been an Empress.

I went to the Pitti in the morning and to the Boboli Gardens in the afternoon.

Thursday, March 31st.

The Albertis came to luncheon. Baroness Strong and Mrs Fisk called in the afternoon. They both asked us all to entertainments, but Housman explained that we had guests ourselves every day. He asked them to dinner on Sunday, but they declined.

Friday, April 1st.

Housman has bought some miniatures by a young artist recommended by Mrs Fairburn. I do not think they are well done, but I am no judge. A. and Mrs Campion left.

Saturday, April 2nd.

Mrs Housman suggested having luncheon in the town and going to Fiesole afterwards, but Housman explained, with some embarrassment, that he had promised to go with Mrs Fairburn to see a studio and to have luncheon with her afterwards.

I leave for London to-night. I am going straight through.

Letter from Guy Cunninghame to Mrs Caryl

VILLA BEAU SITE, MENTONE,

Wednesday, April 6th.

DEAREST ELSIE,

Just a line to say I shall arrive the day after to-morrow, and I can only stay one night. Godfrey Mellor left Florence on Saturday, and George and his sister are on their way back. George was very sad at going—I think he feels it's the end—Mrs Housman and Lady Jarvis are staying on till next Monday, and I think Housman also. What I fore-saw has happened more quickly than I expected. Housman is now the devoted slave of Mrs Fairburn, and she has announced her intention of coming to London in the summer, so this will make fresh complications.

I am having great fun here. The Shamiers are here, I am travelling back with them. I am sorry not to be able to stop more than a night in Paris, but it really is impossible.

I can't dine at the Embassy on Friday, I am dining with the Shamiers that night. But I will come and see you in the morning, and we might do some shops and have luncheon together.

Yrs.

G.

From the Diary of Godfrey Mellor

Monday, April 4th. London.

Back at the office. Tuke came this morning and said A. would not come to the office till to-morrow. Cunninghame does not return until Friday.

Tuesday, April 5th.

A. came to the office. He says that Housman has returned to London, but that Mrs Housman and Lady Jarvis will not be back before next Tuesday.

Thursday, April 7th.

Dined with Aunt Ruth. I sat next to a Mrs de la Poer. She told me she knew the Housmans. I said I had been staying with them in Florence. She said: "I suppose Lord Ayton was there." I said that A. and his sister always spent Easter in Italy. She said: "And he spends the summer in Cornwall when Mrs Housman is there. It is extraordinary how far virtuous Roman Catholics will go." I said Mrs Housman was an old friend of mine and I preferred not to discuss her. She said: "Ah, you are right to be loyal to your Chief, but all London knows about it." I changed the subject.

Thursday, April 14th.

Mrs Housman has put off coming till next week. Lady Jarvis spoke to me on the telephone.

Wednesday, April 20th.

Mrs Housman returned on Monday. She has asked me to dinner on Sunday.

Thursday, April 28th.

A. dined with Aunt Ruth. I went there after dinner. Uncle Arthur told us he thought A. would go far, but he thinks he is in the army. A. is going to the country on Saturday.

Friday, April 29th.

Dined with Lady Jarvis. The Housmans were there, and Cunninghame. Cunninghame told me as we walked home that he had seen Housman with a party of people at the Carlton last night. Mrs Fairburn was among them. He says it is a great pity A. does not go out more. It annoys people. I told him A. had dined with Aunt Ruth last night.

The Housmans are not staying long in London. They have taken the same house they had last year on the Thames near Staines. Housman can go up every day to his office as it is so close to London.

Saturday, April 30th.

Dined with Cunninghame. He is staying in London this Sunday. I asked him if he thought A. was likely to marry. He said: "Not yet."

Sunday, May 1st.

Dined with the Housmans. Cunninghame was there, Mrs Fairburn and Miss Housman. After dinner Mrs Fairburn asked Mrs Housman to sing. She said she remembered her singing in America. Mrs Housman sang a few Scotch ballads. Then Miss Housman played. The Housmans are letting their London house for the season. They go down to their house on the Thames at the end of this week. Housman told me I must come down often.

Mrs Fairburn was very gushing about Mrs Housman's singing. I do not think she is very musical.

Letter from Guy Cunninghame to Mrs Caryl

LONDON,

Monday, May 2nd.

DEAREST ELSIE,

I have got two pieces of news for you. Ralph Logan proposed to Lavinia Wray and she has refused him. I don't think you know him; he is in the army. But he is Sir Walter Logan's heir and will inherit, besides a lot of London property, a most beautiful old house in Essex, Tudor. Besides that, he is charming and has been devoted to her for years. This is for you only, of course. He told me himself. He has just come back from India, where he has been for five years. The first thing he did was to fly to Lavinia, who has come back from France and is now in London. He came to see me yesterday afternoon and told me all about it. I said something about her perhaps changing her mind if he was persistent. He said there was no chance of this, he felt sure. Lavinia told him she would never marry, and she said she was not going out after this year. I believe she is going to be a nurse. She used to talk of this some time ago. The second piece of news is that George has been offered to be Governor of Madras. That is also a secret, of course. I don't know whether he will accept it or not. Sir Henry, who is George's godfather, is, George tells me, tremendously keen about his accepting it.

I don't think he has been seeing much of the Housmans since she has been back. She only came back last week. I don't think she wants to see him. I dined there on Sunday. There was no one there except that extremely tiresome Mrs Fairburn, who now does what she likes with Housman. They are not going to be in London during the summer at all and are letting their house.

Yrs.

G.

From the Diary of Godfrey Mellor

Monday, May 2nd.

Mrs Shamier has asked me to dinner next Thursday. The invitation surprised me as I scarcely know her.

Tuesday, May 3rd.

A. asked me to luncheon to meet Sir Henry St Clair. Sir Henry is an old man, over seventy, with very strong views and a fiery temper. He is his godfather. Mrs Campion was there. He lives in Scotland and said he had not been to London for the last five years. But he said he was enjoying himself and meant to go to the Derby. He looks surprisingly young for his age, not more than sixty.

Wednesday, May 4th.

Went with the Housmans to hear the Gilbert & Sullivan Company at Hammersmith: *Patience;* we enjoyed it greatly. *Patience* is a classic. The performance was adequate. My enjoyment was marred by the comments of Mrs Fairburn, who went with us. She said she thought it *vieux jeu*, and preferred Debussy: a foolish comparison.

Thursday, May 5th.

I dined with the Shamiers. They live in Upper Brook Street. Mrs Vaughan, whom I had met staying with Lady Jarvis, was there; a young Guardsman and a Miss Ivy Hollystrop, an American, who, I believe, is a beauty.

I sat next to Mrs Shamier. She asked me where I had spent Easter. I told her. She said she did not know the Housmans, but had heard a great deal about her. Cunninghame had told her that she sang quite divinely. I said that Mrs Housman had received a very sound musical education. She asked me what kind of man Housman was. I said he was a very generous man and did a lot for charities. She asked me if I had known them a long time. I said yes, a long time. She said she remembered Walter Bell's picture perfectly and if it was at all like her she must be a very beautiful woman. I said it was generally considered to be a faithful portrait. She asked me if the Housmans bad any children. I said no. Mrs Shamier said she would like to meet Mrs Housman very much, but she understood they did not go out much. I said they were living in the country.

Friday, May 6th.

I dined with Lady Jarvis. She was alone. She asked me to spend Sunday week with her in the country. She told me that Sir Henry St Clair had gone back to Scotland, much displeased. He has had a difference with A. He is, she said, a very dictatorial man.

Saturday, May 7th.

Went down to the Housmans' villa on the Thames. Mrs Fairburn was there, but no other guests. Mrs Fairburn asked Mrs Housman to sing after dinner, but she declined.

Sunday, May 8th.

Mrs Fairburn and Housman went out on the river. I sat with Mrs Housman in the garden. She read aloud from Chateaubriand's *René*. It sounded, as she read it, very fine.

Letter from Guy Cunninghame to Mrs Caryl

LONDON,

Monday, May 9th.

DEAREST ELSIE,

George has refused Madras. Sir Henry, who had heard about the offer from H., who is an intimate friend of his, came up post haste from Scotland. He told George he *must* accept it. George said he would think it over, and did so for forty-eight hours, then he made up his mind, and he settled to refuse it. Sir Henry stormed and raved and said it would have broken George's father's heart if he had been alive, but it was no use. George was as obstinate as a mule. He said he liked his present work and he did not want to leave England. Sir Henry went straight back to Scotland.

The Housmans have left. I spent Sunday at Rosedale with Lady Jarvis. She says that Mrs Fairburn is always there and was staying there this Saturday Quite apart from anything else she is a very tiresome woman. But she is no fool. In Housman she had found a gold-mine.

The Shamiers are back. I am dining there next week. George is depressed. He is fond of old Sir H. and doesn't like having annoyed him. Sir H. says he will never forgive him. I can't understand why people can't let other people lead their own lives.

The *Compagnie de Cristal* haven't sent my little chandelier. If you are passing that way could you ask about it?

Yrs.

G.

From the Diary of Godfrey Mellor

Monday, May 9th.

I was trying to remember the date a French colonel had called at the office, and I consulted Tuke. He did not remember, but said he would refer to his diary. I asked him if he kept a diary regularly. He said he had kept his diary without missing a day for the last five years, but he always burnt it every New Year's Day.

Tuesday, May 10*th.*

A. asked me to dinner. He said he very seldom saw the Housmans now, but Housman had asked him to stay there on Sunday week. He was going next Sunday to Rosedale. He told me he had been offered the Governorship of Madras, and had refused it. He said he could not live in tropical climates. They made him ill. He said he hated the summer in London. He would have a lot of tedious dinners. There were several next week he would be obliged to go to.

Wednesday, May 11*th.*

I dined with Cunninghame. He talked of the Madras appointment, and said it was absurd offering it to A. The tropics made him ill. He was ill even in Egypt. He said Housman had a small flat in London, where he stays during the week.

Thursday, May 12*th.*

Cunninghame dined at Aunt Ruth's. I went after dinner. So did A. I could see Aunt Ruth was pleased. Uncle Arthur confused Cunninghame with A. and congratulated C. on his answers in the House of Lords.

Friday, May 13*th.*

Lady Jarvis gave a small musical party, which was what I call a large musical party. Someone sang Russian songs, and Bernard Sachs played Mozart on the harpsichord. It would have been very enjoyable had there not been such a crowd. Housman was there, but not Mrs Housman.

Saturday, May 14*th. Rosedale.*

Went down to Staines this afternoon. Mrs Housman, A., Cunninghame, Miss Macdonald, and Mrs Campion were there. Housman was expected and had told Mrs Housman he was coming by a later train, but he sent a telegram saying he had been detained in London.

Sunday, May 15*th. Rosedale.*

It poured with rain all day, so we sat indoors. Mrs Housman played and sang. She drove to church in the morning in a shut fly.

Letter from Guy Cunninghame to Mrs Caryl

LONDON,

Monday, May 16*th.*

DEAREST ELSIE,

I have just come back from Rosedale, where we had a most amusing Sunday, rather spoilt by the incessant rain. Of course it cleared up *this* morning, and it's now a glorious day. The Housmans were asked and she came, and he was expected by a later train, but chucked at the last minute. Nobody was there except Mrs Campion, Freda, and Godfrey.

We had a lot of music. Mrs Housman never let George have one moment's conversation with her. He is quite miserable. It is quite clear that she has cut him out of her life. I think it would have been better if he had gone to Madras. It's too late now, they've appointed someone else.

Last Tuesday I went to a huge dinner-party at Lady Arthur Mellor's, Godfrey's aunt. Sir Arthur is quite gaga and took me for George the whole evening. I sat between an English blue stocking and the wife of one of the Russian secretaries. She told me rather pointedly that these were the kind of people she preferred. "Ici," she said, "on voit de vrais Anglais, des gens vraiment bien." There was no gainsaying that.

But of course the chief news, which you probably have heard, is that Louise Shamier has left her husband, and she is going to marry Lavroff—that is to say, if she gets a divorce. He apparently refused to do the necessary in the way of making a divorce possible, so she has left him and has gone to Italy with Lavroff. Everybody thinks it is the greatest pity, and I, personally, am miserable about it. The only comfort is that it might have been George.

Yrs.

G.

From the Diary of Godfrey Mellor

Monday, May 16th.

Caught a bad cold at Rosedale from walking in the wet.

Tuesday, May 17th.

Cold worse. Saw the doctor, who said I must go to bed and not think of going to the office.

Wednesday, May 18th.

Stayed in bed all day and read a book called *Sir Archibald Malmaison,* by Julian Hawthorne.

Thursday, May 19th.

Better. Got up.

Friday, May 20th.

Went to the office.

Saturday, May 21st.

Went down to Staines to the Housmans'. Found Lady Jarvis, A. and Mrs Fairburn. At dinner Mrs Fairburn talked of the Shamier divorce. Mrs Housman said she admired people who behaved like that, and she thought it far better than a hidden liaison. Mrs Fairburn agreed, and said there was nothing she despised so much as dishonesty and concealment.

Sunday, May 22nd.

It again rained all Sunday, so we were unable to go on the river. It cleared up in the evening. Housman took Mrs Fairburn out in a punt.

Housman told us he had taken for the summer the same house they had last year at Carbis Bay. He invited A. to come there and to stay as long as he liked. A. said he would be yachting on the west coast this summer and he would certainly pay them a visit. Housman said Lady Jarvis must come, and he is going to ask Cunninghame. Mrs Fairburn said it was a pity she would not be able to come, but she always spent August and September in France.

Monday, May 23rd.

I had luncheon with Cunninghame at his Club. He said that A. does not seem quite so depressed as usual.

Dined at the Club.

Tuesday, May 24th.

A. is giving a dinner to some French *députés* at his Club. Cunninghame and I have both been invited.

Wednesday, May 25th.

Dined at the Club with Solway. Went to the Opera afterwards, for which Solway had been given two places. Debussy's *Pelléas et Mélisande*. We both enjoyed it.

Thursday, May 26th.

Dined with Aunt Ruth. I had a long talk with her after dinner. She asked after Riley, whom she knows well. "I hear," she said, "he has become a Roman Catholic; of course he will always have a *parti-pris* now. I wonder if he has realised that." Uncle Arthur joined in the conversation and thought we were talking of someone else, but of whom I have no idea, as he said it all came from not going to school. Riley has been to three schools, besides Oxford, Heidelberg and Berlin universities, and has taken his degree in French law. He, Riley, is staying with me to-morrow night.

Friday, May 27th.

I told Riley that I had heard a lady discussing his conversion lately, and that she had wondered whether he realised that he would have a *parti-pris* in future. Riley said: "I rather hope I shall. Do you really think one becomes a Catholic to drift like a sponge on a sea of indecision, or to be like an Æolian harp? Don't you yourself think," he said, "that *parti-pris* is rather a mild term for such a tremendous decision, such a *venture*? Would your friend think *parti-pris* the right expression to use of a man who nailed his colours to the mast during a sea-battle? It is a good example of *miosis*." I asked him what *miosis* meant. He said that if I wanted another example it would be miosis to say that the French Revolution put Marie Antoinette to considerable inconvenience. Besides which, it was putting the cart before the horse to say you would be likely to have a *parti-pris,* when by the act of becoming a Catholic you had proclaimed the greatest of all possible *parti-pris*. It was like saying to a man who had enlisted in the Army: "You will probably become very pro-British." "You won't," he said, "think things out." I said that it was not I who had made the comment, but my aunt, Lady Mellor.

Saturday, May 28th.

A. has gone to the country. Dined at the Club.

Sunday, May 29th.

Had luncheon with Lady Maria. The company consisted of Hollis, the play-wright, and his wife, Miss Flora Routledge, who, I believe, began to write novels in the sixties, Sir Hubert Taylor, the Academician, and his wife, and Sir Horace Main, K.C. I was the only person present not a celebrity.

Lady Maria asked me how the Housmans were. She had not seen them for an age. I said the Housmans were living in the country.

She said I must bring A. to luncheon one Sunday. "Who would he like to meet?" she asked; "I am told he only likes musicians, and I am so unmusical, I know so few. But perhaps he only likes beautiful musicians." I said I was sure A. would be pleased to meet anyone she asked. She said: "I'm sure it's no use asking him; he's sure to be away on Sundays." I said A. usually spent Sunday at Littlehampton. "Or on the Thames," Lady Maria said.

She said she hadn't seen the Housmans for a year. She heard Mr Housman had dropped all his old friends.

Letter from Guy Cunninghame to Mrs Caryl

Monday, May 30th.

DEAREST ELSIE,

I have been terribly bad about writing, and I haven't written to you for a fortnight. I got your letter last week, and was immensely amused by all you say. Sunday week I stayed with Edith, a family party, but rather fun all che same. I went to the opera twice this week and once the week before. Nothing very exciting. The Housmans haven't got a box this year. Yesterday I stayed with them at Staines. There was no one else there except Miss Housman. Thank heaven, no Mrs Fairburn! George, by the way, hasn't the remotest idea of "Bert's" infidelities. I believe he thinks him a model husband. He is still in low spirits, but rather better because he is fearfully busy. He has been going out more lately, which is a good thing, and he has been entertaining foreigners and official people, too. People are now saying he is going to marry Lavinia Wray That story has only just reached the large public. They are a little bit out of date. As a matter of fact, Lavinia has quite settled to go in for nursing, but she hasn't broken it yet to her relations. Louise will, I believe, get her divorce. They have left Italy and gone to Russia, where Lavroff has got a large property.

I have got a terribly busy week next week, dinners nearly every night, besides balls. So don't be surprised if you don't hear from me for some time.

Yrs.

G.

From the Diary of Godfrey Mellor

Monday, May 30th.

Heard to-day from Gertrude. She and Anstruther arrive next week for three months' leave from Buenos Aires. They are going to stay at the Hans Crescent Hotel. Anstruther does not expect to go back to Buenos Aires. They hope to get Christiania or Belgrade. They ask me to inform Aunt Ruth and Uncle Arthur of their arrival, which I must try to remember to do, as Gertrude is Aunt Ruth's favourite niece.

Tuesday, May 31st.

A. is not at all well. He says he has got a bad headache, but he has to go to an official dinner to-night. He is also most annoyed at having been chosen as a delegate to the Conference that takes place in Canada in August. This, he says, will prevent his doing any yachting this year as he will not be back before the end of September.

Wednesday, June 1st.

Riley came to see me at the office and asked me whether I could put him up for a few nights. I would with pleasure, but I warned him that I should be having most of my meals with Solway, who is up in London for a week.

Thursday, June 2nd.

Went to Aunt Ruth's after dinner and remembered to tell her that Gertrude was arriving next week. Aunt Ruth was glad to hear the news and said she hoped Edmund would get promotion this time. He had been passed over so often. I said I hoped so also, but I suppose I did not display enough enthusiasm, as Aunt Ruth said I didn't seem to take much interest in my brother-in-law's career. I assured her I was fond of Gertrude and had the greatest respect for my brother-in-law. Uncle Arthur said: "What, Anstruther? The man's a pompous ass." Aunt Ruth was rather shocked.

Friday, July 3rd.

Solway has arrived in London. He is staying at St Leonard's Terrace, Chelsea. He is taking me to a concert to-morrow night. Riley has also arrived. He said he would prefer not to go to a concert.

Saturday, June 4th.

The concert last night was a success. Miss Bowden played Bach's *Chaconne.* Solway was greatly excited and said loudly: "I knew she could do it; I knew she could do it."

Sunday, June 5th.

A. hasn't been at all well this week, and he has put off staying with the Housmans to-day. They asked me, but as Solway and Riley were here I did not like to go. Cunninghame has asked me to dinner next week to meet his cousin, Mrs Caryl. I shall have to conceal from Gertrude that I am going to meet them, as Caryl was promoted over his head and she would think it disloyal on my part. Solway and Riley had luncheon with me at the Club. In the afternoon I went to hear Miss Bowden play at a Mrs Griffith's house, where Solway is staying. We could not persuade Riley to come. I had supper there with Solway. Riley went to more literary circles and had supper with Professor Langdon, the Shakespearean critic.

Letter from Guy Cunninghame to Mrs Caryl

LONDON,

Monday, June 6th.

DEAREST ELSIE,

Please write down in your engagement book that you are dining with me on Thursday as well as on Monday. I have asked Godfrey Mellor to meet you on Thursday. George is laid up with appendicitis, and I am afraid he is *very* bad indeed. The doctors are going to decide to-day whether they are to operate immediately or not. He is at a nursing home in Welbeck Street. His sister is looking after him. He was going to Canada in August. I don't suppose he will be able to now.

I am looking forward to seeing you quite tremendously.

Yours,

G.

From the Diary of Godfrey Mellor

Monday, June 6th.

A. has got appendicitis and has been taken to a nursing home. I have just heard he is to have an operation to-morrow morning.

Tuesday, June 7th.

A.'s operation was successfully performed, but he is still very ill. Cunninghame has been to Welbeck Street this morning and saw his sister. She is most anxious. He was, of course, not allowed to see A.

Wednesday, June 8th.

I sat up late last night talking to Riley.

Thursday, June 9th.

Cunninghame went to Welbeck Street and saw the doctor. He says there is every chance of his recovery. Apparently the danger was in having to do the operation at once, while there was still inflammation. It was not exactly appendicitis, but Cunninghame's report was too technical for my comprehension.

I dined with Cunninghame to-day to meet Mrs Caryl. I had not met her husband before. He is, I thought, slightly stiff. Lady Jarvis was there also. She was much disturbed about A.'s illness.

Friday, June 10th.

Gertrude and Edmund Anstruther arrived yesterday. I dined with them to-night. Edmund said the way diplomats were treated was a scandal. The hard-working members of the profession were always passed over. The best posts were given to men outside the profession. No conscientious man could expect to get on in such a profession. If he was passed over this time he would not stand it any longer, but he would leave the Service altogether. The Foreign Office, he said, was so weak. They never backed up a subordinate who took a strong line. They always climbed down. I wondered what Edmund had been taking a strong line about in Buenos Aires. Gertrude agreed. She said they had been there for three years without leave, and if they did not get a good post she would advise Edmund to retire and get something in the City. There were plenty of firms in the city who would jump at getting Edmund. She mentioned the Housmans and said she knew they were friends of mine, and didn't want to say anything against them, but she had met many people in Buenos Aires who knew Mrs Housman intimately, and said she was rather a dangerous woman. I asked in what way she was dangerous. Gertrude said: "Perhaps you do not know she is a Roman Catholic." I said I had known this for years, but she never talked of it. "That's just what I mean," said Gertrude; "they are far too subtle, and I am afraid too underhand to talk of it openly. They lead you on." I asked Gertrude if she thought Mrs Housman wished to convert me. She said most certainly. Her friends in Buenos Aires had told her she had made many converts. It was the only thing she cared for, and even if she didn't, Roman Catholics were obliged to do so. It was only natural, if they thought we all went to hell if we were not converted.

I said I was not sure Roman Catholics did believe that. Gertrude and Edmund said I was wrong. I could ask anyone. Gertrude repeated she had no wish to say anything against Mrs Housman, and she was convinced she was a good woman according to her lights.

Edmund said there had been many conversions in the Diplomatic Service. He was convinced this was part of a general conspiracy. If you wanted to get on in the Diplomatic Service you had better be a Roman Catholic. Of course those who did not choose to sacrifice their conscience, their independence, their traditions, and were loyal to the Church and the State, suffered. I said I didn't quite see where loyalty to the State came in. Edmund said: "How could you be loyal to the State when you were under the authority of an Italian Bishop?" I must know that the Italian Cardinals were always in the majority. I said that, considering the number of Catholics in England, compared with the number of Catholics in other countries, I should be surprised to see a majority of English Cardinals at the Vatican. I said Edmund wanted England to be a Protestant country, and at the same time to have the lion's share in Catholic affairs. Edmund said that was not at all what he meant. What he meant was that an Englishman should be loyal to his Church, which was an integral part of the State.

I said there were many Englishmen who would prefer the State to have nothing to do with the Church. Edmund said there were many Englishmen who did not deserve the name of Englishmen. For instance, Caryl, who was now Second Secretary at Paris, had been promoted over his head three years ago. What was the reason? Mrs Caryl was a Roman Catholic and Caryl had been converted soon after his marriage. I foolishly said that the Caryls were now in London, and when Edmund asked me how I knew this I said that Aunt Ruth had told me.

This raised a storm, as it appears that Aunt Ruth does know the Caryls and asks them to dinner when they are in London. Edmund said he would talk to Aunt Ruth about them seriously. I asked him as a favour to do no such thing. And Gertrude told him not to be foolish, and added magnanimously that Mrs Caryl was a nice woman, if a little fast.

For a man who has lived all his life abroad Edmund Anstruther is singularly deeply imbued with British prejudice.

They are staying in London until the middle of July. Then they are going on a round of visits. Edmund is confident that he will get Christiania. I feel that it is more than doubtful.

Riley went back to Shelborough to-day.

Saturday, June 11th.

Received a telegram from Housman, asking me to go to Staines. I went down by the afternoon train, and found Lady Jarvis, Miss Housman and Carrington-Smith. Housman was anxious for news of A. I told him I believed he was now out of danger, but that it would be a long time before he was quite well again. Housman said he must certainly come to Cornwall. I said he had intended to go to Canada for a Conference, but would be unable to do so now. Housman said that was providential.

Sunday, June 12th.

A fine day, but the river was crowded and hardly enjoyable. I sat with Mrs Housman in the garden in the evening. The others went on the river again. Mrs Housman asked me if I had seen A. I said he was not allowed to see anyone.

Monday, June 13th.

A. is getting on as well as can be expected. There appears to be no doubt of his recovery. Cunninghame is going to see him to-day.

Tuesday, June 12th.

Cunninghame says that A. wants to see me. I am to go there to-morrow.

Dined with Hope, who was at Oxford with me. He is just back from Russia, where he has been to make arrangements for producing some play in London. He thinks of nothing now but the stage, and a play of his is going to be produced at the Court Theatre. I promised to go and see it. He spoke of Riley, and I told him he had become a Roman Catholic. Hope said he regarded that as sinning against the light. He said no one *at this time of day* could believe such things.

Wednesday, June 15th.

I went to see A. at Welbeck Street. He has been very ill and looks white and thin. His sister was there, but I had some conversation with him alone. I told him all the news I could think of, which was not much. He said he liked seeing people, but was not allowed more than one visitor a day. He had got a very good nurse. Housman had sent him grapes and magnificent fruit every day. He said he would like to see Mrs Housman, but supposed that was impossible, as she never came to London now. He said Cunninghame had been very good to him, and had put off going to Ascot to look after him.

I wrote to Mrs Housman this evening and gave her A.'s message.

Thursday, June 16th.

Dined with Aunt Ruth. Gertrude and Edmund were there. Edmund said to Aunt Ruth that he had heard the Caryls were in London. Aunt Ruth said she had no idea of this, and she would ask them to dinner next Thursday. Aunt Ruth asked a good many diplomats to meet Edmund, and they had a long talk after dinner about their posts. They called Edmund their "*Cher collègue.*" Edmund enjoyed himself immensely. Uncle Arthur cannot bear him, nor, indeed, any diplomats, and it is, I think, the chief cross of his life that Aunt Ruth asks so many of them to dinner.

Aunt Ruth asked after A. and said that she had been to inquire.

Friday, June 17th.

Received a letter from Mrs Housman, saying she was coming up to London to-morrow, and was going to stay with Lady Jarvis till Monday. She would go and see A. on Sunday afternoon if convenient. She asked me to ring up the nurse and find out. I did so and arranged for her to call at four o'clock.

Saturday, June 18th.

I dined with Lady Jarvis. There was no one there but Mrs Housman and myself. Cunninghame is staying somewhere with friends of the Caryls.

Sunday, June 19th.

I had luncheon with Aunt Ruth. Edmund and Gertrude were there, but no one else. Edmund has been appointed to Berne. It is not what he had hoped, but better than any of us expected. He said Berne might become a most important post in the event of a European war.

Monday, June 20th.

Dined with the Caryls at the Ritz. Cunninghame was there and Miss Hollystrop. Mrs Vaughan asked me whether it was true that A. had become a Roman Catholic. She had heard Mrs Housman had converted him. Cunninghame deftly turned the conversation on account of Mrs Caryl.

We all went to the opera—*Faust.*

Tuesday, June 21st.

I went to see A. He told me Mrs Housman had been to see him. He is still in bed, but looks better.

Wednesday, June 22nd.

Barnes of the F.O. came to the office this morning. He asked after A. He said he had heard that the real cause of his illness was his passion for Mrs Housman, who would have nothing to do with him unless he was converted. Cunninghame said he wondered he could talk such nonsense.

Thursday, June 23rd.

Went to Aunt Ruth's after dinner. The Caryls were there, and Gertrude and Edmund came after dinner. Heated arguments were going on about the situation in Russia, Edmund taking the ultra-conservative point of view, much to the annoyance of Aunt Ruth and Uncle Arthur, who felt even more strongly on the matter because he thought they were discussing the French Revolution.

Friday, June 24th.

Dined with Lady Jarvis; she was alone. She said Mrs Housman was coming up again to-morrow. The fact is, she says, Staines is intolerable now on Sundays. Mrs Fairburn comes down almost every Sunday. She overwhelms Mrs Housman with her gush and her pretended silliness. Housman thinks her the most wonderful woman he has ever met.

Saturday, June 25th.

Went down to S—— to stay with Riley. Riley lives in a small villa surrounded with laurels. A local magnate came to dinner, who is suspected of being about to present some expensive masterpieces to the public gallery.

Sunday, June 26th.

Riley went to Mass in the morning. I sat in his smoking-room, which is a litter of books and papers and exceedingly untidy. A geologist came to luncheon, Professor Langer, a naturalised German. When we were walking in the garden afterwards, he said he could not understand how Riley reconciled his creed with plain facts of geology. But Riley's case surprised him less than that of another of his colleagues, who was a great authority on geology, and nevertheless a devout Catholic, and not only never missed Mass on Sundays, but had told him, Langer, that he fully subscribed to every point of the Catholic Faith. It was true he was an Irishman, but politically he was not at all fanatical, and not even a Home-Ruler.

In the afternoon we had tea with the magnate, whose house is full of Academy pictures. I now understand what happens to that great quantity of pictures we see once at the Academy and then never again.

An art critic was invited to tea also. He had, I believe, been invited here to persuade the magnate in question to present some very modern piece of art to the city. He seemed disappointed when he saw the pictures on the walls, and when the magnate asked his opinion of a composition called *A Love Letter*, he said he did not think the picture a very good one. The magnate said he regretted not having bought *Home Thoughts*, by the same painter, which was undoubtedly superior.

We dined alone, and I told Riley what Professor Langer had said. He said: "Most Protestants, whether they have any religion or not, attribute Protestant notions to the Catholic Church. What these people say shows to what extent the conception of Rome has been distorted by their being saturated with Protestant ideas. Mallock says somewhere that the Anglicans talk of the Catholic Church as if she were a *lapsed Protestant sect*, and they attack her for being false to what she has never professed. He says they don't see the real difference between the two Churches, which is not in this or that dogma, but in the authority on which all dogma rests. The Professors you quote take for granted that Catholics base their religion, as Protestants do, on the Bible *solely*, and judged from that point of view she seems to them superstitious and dishonest. But Catholics believe that Christ guaranteed infallibility to the Church *in perpetuum: perpetual* infallibility. Catholics discover this not *at first* from the Church as doctrine, but from records as trustworthy human documents, and they believe that the Church being perpetually infallible can only interpret the Bible in the right way. They believe she is guided in the interpretation of the Bible by the same Spirit which inspired the Bible. She teaches us *more* about the Bible. She says *this* is what the Bible teaches."

He said: "Mallock makes a further point. It is not only Protestant divines who talk like that. It is your advanced thinkers, men like Langer and his colleagues. They utterly disbelieve in the Protestant religion; they trust the Protestants in nothing else, but at the same time they take their word for it, without further inquiry, that Protestantism is more reasonable than Catholicism. If they have destroyed Protestantism they conclude they must have destroyed Catholicism *a fortiori*. With regard to Langer's geological friend, it doesn't make a pin's difference to a Catholic whether evolution or natural selection is true or false. Neither of these theories pretends to explain the origin of life. Catholics believe the origin of life is God." He had heard a priest say, not long ago: "A Catholic can believe in evolution, and in evolution before evolution, and in evolution before that, if he likes, but what he must believe is that God made the world and in it *mind,* and that at some definite moment the mind of man rebelled against God."

Monday, June 27th.

A. telephoned for me. I saw him this afternoon. His room was full of flowers. He will not be allowed to get up till the end of the week. As soon as he is allowed to go out the doctor says he ought to go away and get some sea air. There is no question of his going to Canada. The Housmans have asked him to go to Cornwall and he is going there as soon as he can. He asked me when I was going. I said at the end of the month, if that would be convenient to him.

Tuesday, June 28th.

Finished Renan's *Souvenirs d'Enfance et de Jeunesse*. He says: "Je regrettais par moments de n'être pas protestant, afin de pouvoir être philosophe sans cesser d'être Chrétien. Puis je reconnaissais qu'il n'y a que les Catholiques qui soient conséquents." Riley's argument. Dined at the Club.

Wednesday, June 29th.

Dined with Hope at a restaurant in Soho. Quite a large gathering, with no one I knew. We had dinner in a private room. Two journalists—Hoxton, who writes in one of the Liberal newspapers, and Brice, who edits a weekly newspaper—had a heated argument about religion. Brice is and has always been an R.C. Hoxton's views seemed to me violent but undefined. He said, as far as I understood, that the Eastern Church was far nearer to early Christian tradition than the Western Church, and that by not defining things too narrowly and by not having an infallible Pope the Greeks had an inexpressible advantage over the Romans. Upon which someone else who was there said that the Greeks believed in the infallibility of the First Seven Councils; they believed their decisions to be as infallible as any papal utterance, and that dogma had been defined once and for all by the Councils. Brice said this was quite true, and while the Greeks had shut the door, the Catholic Church had left the door open. Besides which, he argued, what was the result of the action of the Greeks? Look at the Russian Church. As soon as it was separated it gave birth to another schism and that schism resulted in the rise of about a hundred religions, one of which had for one of its tenets that children should be strangled at their birth so as to inherit the Kingdom of Heaven without delay. That, said Brice, is the result of schism.

The other man said that there was no religion so completely under the control of the Government as the Russian. The Church was ultimately in the hands of gendarmes. Hoxton said that in spite of schisms, and in spite of anything the Government might do, the Eastern Church retained the early traditions of Christianity. Therefore, if an Englishman wanted to become a Catholic, it was absurd for him to become a Roman Catholic. He should first think of joining the Eastern Church and becoming a Greek Catholic. The other man, whose name I didn't catch, asked why, in that case, did Russian philosophers become Catholics and why did Solovieff, the Russian philosopher, talk of the pearl Christianity having unfortunately reached Russia smothered under the dust of Byzantium?

Brice said the Greek Church was schismatic and the Anglican Church was heretical and that was the end of the matter. Hoxton said: "My philosophy is quite as good as yours." Brice said it was a pity he could neither define nor explain his philosophy. Hope, who was bored by the whole argument, turned the conversation on to the Russian stage.

Thursday, June 30th.

Dined with Aunt Ruth. After dinner I sat next to a Russian diplomatist who knew Riley. He said he was glad he had become a Catholic—he himself was Orthodox. He evidently admired the Catholic religion. He said, among other things, how absurd it was to think that such floods of ink had been used to prove the Gospel of St John had not been written by St John. He said, even if it wasn't, the Church has said it was written by St John for over a thousand years. She has made it her own. He himself saw no reason to think it was not written by St John. Uncle Arthur, who caught the tail end of this conversation, said the authorship of *John Peel* was a subject of much dispute. Gertrude wasn't there; they have gone to the country.

Friday, July 1st.

Dined with Lady Jarvis. Cunninghame was there and a large gathering of people. More people came after dinner and there was music, but such a crowd that I could not get near enough to listen so I gave it up and stayed in another room. Lady Jarvis told me Mrs Housman is going down to Cornwall next Monday.

Saturday, July 30th. Grey Farm, Carbis Bay.

Arrived this evening after a hot and disagreeable journey. The Housmans are here alone. Housman goes back to London on Tuesday. A. is coming down here as soon as he is fit to travel. He is still very weak.

Sunday, July 31st.

The Housmans went to Mass. Father Stanway came to luncheon. He said he had been giving instruction to an Indian boy who is being brought up as an R.C. I asked him if it was difficult for an Indian to understand Christian dogma. Father Stanway said that the child had amazed him. He had been telling him about the Trinity and the Indian had said to him: "I see—ice, snow, rain—all water."

Monday, August 1st.

Housman played golf. Mrs Housman took me to the cliffs and began reading out *Les Misérables,* which I have never read.

Tuesday, August 2nd.

Housman left early this morning. We sat on the beach and read *Les Misérables.*

Wednesday, August 3rd.

Lady Jarvis arrives to-morrow. We continued *Les Misérables* in the afternoon and after dinner. Mrs Housman said that some conversations and the reading of certain passages in books were like *events*. Once or twice in her life she had come across sentences in a book which, although they had nothing extraordinary about them and expressed things anyone might have thought or said, were like a revelation, or a solution, and seemed to be written in letters of flame and had a permanent effect on her whole life; one such sentence was the following from *Les Misérables*: "Ne craignons jamais les voleurs ni les meurtriers. Ce sont là les dangers du dehors, les petits dangers. Craignons nous-mêmes. Les préjugés, voila les voleurs; les vices, voila les meurtriers. Les grands dangers sont au dedans de nous. Qu'importe ce qui menace notre tête ou notre bourse!" She said: "Of course this has never prevented me from feeling frightened when I hear a scratching noise in the night. That paralyses me with terror."

Thursday, August 4th.

We continued our reading. The weather has been propitious. Lady Jarvis arrived in the evening. We continued our reading after dinner.

Friday, August 5th.

A. arrived this evening. He was exhausted after the journey and went to bed at once. Housman arrives to-morrow—he is only staying till Monday.

Saturday, August 6th.

A. sat in the garden and Mrs Housman read out some stories by H.G. Wells from a book called *The Plattner Story,* which we all enjoyed.

Housman arrived in the evening. A. is not yet strong enough to walk. He sits in the garden all day. The weather is perfectly suited to an invalid.

Sunday, August 7th.

Housman invited Father Stanway to luncheon. He and Housman talked of politicians and popularity and the Press and to what extent their reputation depended on it. Housman said it was death to a politician not to be mentioned. A politician needed popularity among the public as much as an actor did. Father Stanway said it was a double-edged weapon and that those who lived by it risked perishing by it. Housman said Gladstone and Beaconsfield had lived by it successfully. Father Stanway said it depends whether you want to be famous or whether you want to get things done. A man can do anything in the world if he doesn't mind not getting the credit for it. Father Stanway said nobody realised this better than Lord Beaconsfield. He said somewhere that it was private life that governs the world and that the more you were talked about the less powerful you were.

A. is a little better. I went for a walk with Father Stanway in the afternoon. I asked him a few questions about the system of Confession. He said the Sacrament of Penance was a Divine Institution. I asked him if the practice did not lead to the shirking of responsibility and the dulling of the conscience on the part of those who went to Confession. He said Confession was not an opiate but a sharp and bitter medicine, disagreeable to take but leaving a clean after-taste in the mouth I gave him a hypothetical case of a man being in love with a Catholic married woman. If the woman was a practising Catholic and faithful to her husband, and if she continued to be friends with the man who was in love with her, would she confess her conduct and, if so, would the priest approve of the conduct? Father Stanway said it was difficult to judge unless one knew the whole facts. If the woman knew she was acting in a way which might lead to sin or even to scandal—that is to say, in a way which would have a bad effect on others—she would be bound to confess it. If a woman asked him his advice in such a case he would strongly advise her to put an end to the relationship. I said: "You wouldn't forbid it?" He said: "The Church forbids sin, and penitents when they receive Absolution undertake to avoid the occasions of sin." He said he could not tell me more without knowing more of the facts. Cases were sometimes far more complicated than they appeared to be, but however complicated they were, there was no doubt as to the attitude of the Church towards that kind of sin and to the advisability of avoiding occasions that might bring it about.

Monday, August 8th.

Housman went back to London. Cunninghame arrives to-morrow. A. walked as far as the beach this morning. In the afternoon Lady Jarvis took him for a drive. Mrs Housman went into the town to do some shopping.

Tuesday, August 9th.

We all went for a drive in a motor to a village with a curious name and had tea in a farm-house. Cunninghame arrived in time for dinner. He has been staying at Cowes.

Letter from Guy Cunninghame to Mrs Caryl

CARBIS BAY,

Wednesday, August 10th.

DEAREST ELSIE,

I arrived last night from Cowes. I found Mrs Housman, Lady Jarvis, George and Godfrey.

George is very much better, but he is still weak and can't get about much. He is not allowed to play golf yet. He sits in the garden, and goes for a mild walk once a day. Lady Jarvis says that Mrs Housman is very unhappy. In the first place, her home is intolerable. Mrs Fairburn makes London quite impossible for her. It is a wonder that she is not here, but as Housman is in London there is nothing to be surprised at. In the second place, Lady Jarvis thinks that Mrs Housman would much rather George hadn't come, but she couldn't help it as Housman asked him.

We do things mostly altogether now. I am staying a fortnight, then I go to Worsel for a week and to Edith's till the end of September; then London. Lady Jarvis says that she is sure Mrs Housman will not spend the winter in London.

Write to me here and tell me about the Mont Dore. I have been there once and think it is an appalling place.

Yrs.

G.

From the Diary of Godfrey Mellor

Wednesday, August 10th.

A. has been doing too much, the doctor says, and he is not to be allowed out of the garden for a few days. Mrs Housman and Lady Jarvis take turns in reading to him aloud. We have finished the Wells book and we are now reading *Midshipman Easy*.

Thursday, August 11th.

I went for a walk with Cunninghame. He said his favourite book was *John Inglesant* and was surprised that I had not read it. He has it with him and has lent it to me.

Friday, August 12th.

It rained all day. We spent the day reading aloud.

Saturday, August 13th.

A. is much better and went for a walk with me this morning.

Sunday, August 14th.

Housman was coming down yesterday but telegraphed to say he was detained. Mrs Housman went to Mass. In the afternoon we received a visit from an American who has come here in a yacht and met Cunninghame and myself in the town this morning. His name is Harold C. Jefferson. When I was introduced to him he said he did not quite catch my name. I said my name was "Mellor"; he said: "Lord or Mister?" Cunninghame told him where he was staying and he said he would call—he knew the Housmans in America. He asked us all to go on board his yacht to-morrow. Mrs Housman, Cunninghame and myself accepted. Lady Jarvis said she would stop with A. who is not up to it.

Monday, August 15th.

We had luncheon on board Mr Jefferson's yacht, a large steam vessel. It has on board a piano and an organ, both of which are played by electricity, which is in some respects satisfactory, but the *tempo* of the *Meistersinger* Overture which was performed for us was accelerated out of all recognition.

Tuesday, August 16th.

A Miss Simpson called in the afternoon to ask Mrs Housman to help with some local charity; she lives at the Hotel. She said she found it very inconvenient not being able to go to Church. We wondered what prevented her doing so, but she soon gave us the reason herself. She said that the local clergyman was so low—no eastward position.

A. is much better and went for a walk with Lady Jarvis.

Wednesday, August 17th.

Housman has written to say that he will not be able to come down until late in September. Carrington-Smith is unwell and he is overwhelmed with business. He, Housman, may have to meet a man in Paris.

Thursday, August 18th.

A rainy day. Cunninghame and I went out in spite of the rain.

Friday, August 19th.

Cunninghame played golf with General York.

Saturday, August 20th.

Lady Jarvis, Mrs Housman and myself went for a drive. A. played golf with Cunninghame. I began *John Inglesant* last night. Mrs Housman has never read it. After dinner we had some music. Mrs Housman played Schubert's *Prometheus* and hummed the tune. She says it is a man's song.

Sunday, August 21st.

A. says he is going to have his yacht sent up here—he will be able to sail back in her. Mrs Housman went to Mass. In the afternoon we sat in the garden and read out aloud *Cashel Byron's Profession,* a novel by Bernard Shaw. A. enjoyed it immensely.

Monday, August 22nd.

We drove to the Lizard in a motor and had luncheon at the Hotel. A. misses his yacht very much but he has sent for her. After dinner we played Clumps.

Tuesday, August 23rd.

Cunninghame was going to-morrow but he is staying till Saturday. Mrs Housman went to Newquay to the convent for the day. Lady Jarvis took A. for a drive.

Wednesday, August 24th.

This morning A., Cunninghame and myself walked down to the town. We met a friend of Cunninghame's called Randall, who is yachting. He has just come from France.

Letter from Guy Cunninghame to Mrs Caryl

GREY FARM, CARBIS BAY,

Thursday, August 25th.

DEAREST ELSIE,

I am stopping here till Saturday, then Worsel, then Edith's. You had better write to Edith's. Yesterday morning we were in the town, George, Godfrey and I, and we met Jimmy Randall, who has come here in the Goldberg's yacht. They had been to St Malo and other places in France. When we said we were staying with the Housmans, Randall said there was not much chance of our seeing Housman for some time as he was having the time of his life with Mrs Fairburn at a little place near Deauville.

This came as a revelation to George, who had no idea of Housman's adventures. He has scarcely spoken since. We are having a very happy time and I am miserable at having to go away. George is quite well. He has sent for his yacht, but he is not staying on very long as he has got to go to one or two places before he goes back to London. The weather has been divine. Godfrey is quite cheerful.

I shan't write again till I get to Edith's. I shan't stop more than a night at Worsel on the way.

Edith is clamouring for me to come. The Caryls are staying there.

Yrs.

G.

From the Diary of Godfrey Mellor

Thursday, August 25th.

I went out for a walk with Cunninghame; he asked me whether I had liked *John Inglesant*. I said I had it read with interest but it gave me the creeps; it had the chill of a dream world; I preferred the character of Eustace Inglesant to that of his brother John. Cunninghame said he had read it five times; that *John Inglesant*, Flaubert's *Trois Contes* and Anthony Hope's *The King's Mirror* were his three favourite books. I had read neither of the others. Mrs Housman and A. went for a walk in the afternoon. After dinner Lady Jarvis read out a story by Stevenson.

Friday, August 26th.

Mrs Housman went to the town in the afternoon. A. and Cunninghame played golf. I went for a walk with Lady Jarvis. She talked about Mrs Housman. She said it was wonderful what comfort she (Mrs H.) found in her religion. As far as she herself was concerned, she had never ceased to appreciate the luxury of not going to church on Sunday, so much had she disliked being made to go to church before she was grown up. I said Mrs Housman had told me that Roman Catholic children enjoyed going to church. She said: "Yes, and their grown-up people too. Clare will probably go to church this afternoon. If I was a Catholic I could understand it." She said it was the only religion she could understand. "Unhappily to be a Catholic," she said, "one must believe. I am not talking of the ritual and the discipline—I mean one must *believe*, have faith in the supernatural, and I have none." She said that she thought religion was an instinct. Her religion consisted in trying not to hurt other people's feelings. That was difficult enough. She said she had once come across this phrase in a French book: "Aimez-vous les uns les autres, c'est beaucoup dire supportez-vous les uns les autres, c'est déjà assez difficile." Some people, she said, arrived at religion by disbelieving in disbelief. She didn't believe in dogmatic *disbelief but* that didn't lead *her* to anything positive. She said she was glad for Mrs Housman that she had her religion. I asked her if she thought Mrs Housman was very unhappy. She said: "Yes; but there comes a moment in unhappiness when people realise that they must either live, or die. Clare passed that moment a long time ago." People often made God in their own image. Mrs Housman had a beautiful character. She, Lady Jarvis, had no stuff in her to project a deity with. She thought that religion seldom affected conduct. She thought Mrs Housman would have been just the same if she had been brought up as a free-thinker or a Presbyterian. She thought her marriage and her whole life had been a gigantic mistake. She ought, she said, to have been a professional singer. She was an artist by nature. I said I was struck by Mrs Housmans strong common-sense and her tact in dealing with people. "That would have made her all the greater as an artist," Lady Jarvis said. "In all arts you want to be good at other things besides that art. Riding needs mind." She said it was no good wishing to be otherwise but she thought it was very tragic. She said: "If I believed there was another life, this sort of thing wouldn't matter, but as I don't it matters very much." I said it struck me the other way round. If one didn't believe in a future life I didn't see that anything could matter very much. I asked her if she positively believed there wasn't another life. She said: "I don't know. I only know I don't believe in a future life." I asked her if that wasn't faith. She said very possibly, but she at any rate hadn't the fervent faith in no-God that some atheists had. In any case she was not intolerant about it. I asked her if it had not often struck her that agnostics and free-thinkers were still more intolerant than religious people and that they had least business to be. She said that was exactly what she had meant. The religion of other people irritated them; they wanted people to share their particular form of unbelief. She never did that. She thought dogmatic disbelief intolerable. She had the greatest respect for Catholics and would give anything to be able to be one. Mrs Housman never spoke about her religion. We talked about reading. I said I always read the newspapers or rather *The Times* every day. I had done so for fifteen years. She said she never did except in the train but she knew the news as well as I did. We talked about what is good reading for the train and about journeys. I told her of a journey I had once taken in France in a third-class carriage. She said it was lucky one forgot physical discomfort at once unlike mental discomfort. She said something about the appalling unnaturalness of people when they had to deal with death, and then of the misery in seeing other people suffer, of the hardness of some people, and of a book she had just been reading, called *Katzensteg*, by Sudermann, and then of Germans, and so, to music, of Housman's great undeveloped musical talent, of Jews, how favourable the mixture of Jewish and German blood was to music. I said something about Jews being rarely men of creation or action. She said they were just as persistent in getting what they wanted as men of action, so she supposed that it came to the same. Disraeli was a man of action, she supposed, and all the great socialists, Marx and Lassalle, they got what they wanted. "Un de nous a voulu être Dieu et il l'a été," she said a Jewish financier had once said. This led her to Heine. He was her favourite writer, both in prose and verse. Had I ever read his prose? I ought to read *Geschichte der Religion und Philosophie in Deutschland.* It was the most brilliant book of criticism she knew. It was the Jews who had invented all great religions, and socialism was the invention of the Jews. Some people said the Russian revolution was Jewish in idea and leadership and might very likely lead to a new political creed. She said she hated anti-Semitism. This led us to Christianity. Christianity to her meant Catholicism. She could not understand any other form of it. She thought there was nothing in the world more silly than attempts to make a religion of Christianity without the Church—there could only be one Church. "But," I said, "you disbelieve in it." She said: "Yes; but the only thing that could tempt me to believe in it is the continued existence of the Catholic Church." She said: "It's there; it's a fact, whether one believes in its divine origin, as Clare does, or whether one doesn't, as I don't. It must either all hang together or not exist. You can't take a part of it and make a satisfactory and reasonable religion." Not only that, nothing seemed to her more foolish than the attempts to make a religion of Christianity without the Divine element, in which Christ was only a very good man. I said if she did not believe in the divinity of Christ the story could be nothing more to her than a fable. She said: "If one only regards it as a fable, as I suppose I do—but again I have no dogmatic disbelief in it—it is still the most beautiful, impressive, wonderful and tragic story ever invented and it seems to me to lose its whole point if Christ was only a man with hypnotic powers and a head turned by ambition or illusion." She quoted a Frenchman, who had said that he adored Jesus Christ as his Lord and God, but "s'il n'est qu'un homme je préfère Hannibal." Napoleon too had said that he knew men and Jesus Christ was not a man. Regarded as a story the whole point and beauty of the Gospel were lost in all modern versions, rewritings, explanations and interpretations, and none of them held together. She said it was as if one rewrote the fairy tales and made the fairies not fairies but only clever conjurers. By this time we had reached home.

Saturday, August 27th.

Cunninghame went away early this morning. Mrs Housman told me that she was not going to spend the winter in London; she was going to Florence, and it was possible she might be away for a whole year. A. went out this afternoon with Lady Jarvis.

Sunday, August 28th.

Mrs York called in the afternoon. Mrs Housman was out with A. Lady Jarvis and myself entertained her. She was most affable and not at all stiff, as she was last year. She said she had known several of A.'s relations in India. As she went away she said to Lady Jarvis, in the hall: "You never told me Mrs Housman was an *American*—that makes *all* the difference."

Monday, August 29th.

We all went to the Land's End for the day.

Tuesday, August 30th.

A.'s yacht has arrived. We had luncheon on board and went for a short sail in the afternoon; the sea was reasonably smooth, but Lady Jarvis said that the sea under any conditions gave her a headache.

Wednesday, August 31st.

Mrs Housman and A. went out for a sail in the morning and came back for tea. A. says he will have to go away in a day or two. After dinner Mrs Housman read out Burnand's *Happy Thoughts*.

Thursday, September 1st.

A rainy day. Mrs Housman called on Mrs York and has asked her and the General to luncheon next Sunday. I went out for a walk in the rain by myself and got very wet. Mrs Housman said that the Indian servant stood motionless behind Mrs York's chair during the whole of the visit. This embarrassed her. She felt inclined to draw him into the conversation.

Friday, September 2nd.

Mrs Housman went to the convent by herself. Lady Jarvis and A. went out for a walk and I stayed at home. It is quite fine again. A. leaves next Monday.

Saturday, September 3rd.

A. wanted to go out sailing but Mrs Housman thought it was too windy. We all went for a drive instead.

Sunday, September 4th.

General York and Mrs York came to luncheon. The General was a little nervous, but Mrs York was affable and friendly. She said she had never got used to the English climate. Lady Jarvis asked Mrs York if she had been to church. Mrs York said they had a church quite close to their house in the village but she always drove to our village church, although it was three miles off. She could not go to their church as she did not approve of the clergyman's ritualistic practices. He used white vestments at Easter, changed the order of the service, and allowed a picture in church. All that, of course, made it impossible. They went away soon after luncheon. I went for a walk with Lady Jarvis. After dinner A. asked Mrs Housman to sing, but she said she would rather read. She read *Happy Thoughts* aloud.

Monday, September 5th.

A. left in his yacht. He said he would be back in London by the first of October. He is stopping at Plymouth on the way.

Tuesday, September 6th.

Mrs Housman asked me if I had finished *Les Misérables*. I said I had not gone on with it. She read aloud from it in the afternoon.

Wednesday, September 7th.

I leave to-morrow to stay with Aunt Ruth. I have to be in London on the 19th. Lady Jarvis went to the village, we stayed in the garden. After dinner, Mrs Housman sang some Schubert. She leaves Cornwall at the end of the month and then goes to Florence, where she stays rill Easter or perhaps longer.

Monday, October 3rd. London, Gray's Inn.

Cunninghame and A. both came back to-day. Cunninghame asked me to dine with him to-morrow.

Tuesday, October 4th.

Dined with Cunninghame alone in his flat. He said that he knew I had some R.C. friends, perhaps I knew a priest. I said the only priest I had ever spoken to was Father Stanway at Carbis Bay. He said he wanted to consult a priest about certain rules in the R.C. Church. He wanted to know under what conditions a marriage could be annulled. A friend of his wanted a married woman to get her marriage annulled as her husband was living with someone else. He wanted to know whether the marriage could be annulled. I said I knew who he was talking about. He said he had meant me to know. He had promised A. to find out from a priest. A. had been told by her that it was out of the question to get the marriage annulled. It had been a marriage entered into by her own free will and performed with every necessary condition of validity. Of course she was very young when she was married and didn't know what she was doing, but that had nothing to do with it. Her aunt and the nuns in the convent where she had been brought up had thought it was an excellent marriage, as he was well off and a Catholic. Cunninghame begged me to go and see a priest. I said I did not know how this was done. I suggested his asking his cousin, Mrs Caryl. He said she was in Paris and that would be no use, it would not satisfy A. I said I would think about it.

Wednesday, October 5th.

I asked Tuke where and how one could find a priest who would be able to tell one the rules of the Church with regard to marriage. Tuke said any of the Fathers at Farm Street or the Oratory. In the afternoon I went to the Oratory, sent in my card and asked to see a priest. I sat in a little waiting-room downstairs. Presently a tall man came in with very bright eyes and a face with nothing but character left in it. I told him I had come for a friend. It was a case of divorce, or rather of annulment. I knew his Church did not tolerate divorce. I was, myself, not a Catholic. It was the case of a lady, a Catholic, who had married a Catholic. The husband had always been unfaithful and was now almost openly living with someone else. Could the marriage be annulled? The priest asked whether she desired the marriage to be annulled. I told him she had said it was impossible. He asked whether the marriage had been performed under all conditions of validity. I said I did not myself know what these conditions were, but that she had expressly said that the marriage had been performed with her own free will, with every necessary condition of validity. I knew she thought it was out of the question to think of the marriage being annulled, but there was someone who was most devoted to her and wanted to marry her, and he was not satisfied with her saying it was impossible. He wanted the decision confirmed by a priest and that was why I had come. The priest said he was afraid from what I had told him that it was no use thinking of annulment. It was clear from what I had said she knew quite well the conditions that make it possible to apply for the annulment of a marriage. He said he was sure it was a hard case. If I liked he would lend me a book which went into the matter in detail. I said I would not trouble him. It would be enough that I had seen him and heard this from him. I then went away. I went straight back to the office and told C. the result of my visit. He was most grateful to me for having done this. He said he was dining with A. to-night. He said A. was in a terrible state.

Thursday, October 6th.

Cunninghame told me that he had dined with A. and given him the information I had procured for him. He said A. was wretched. Mrs Housman arrives in London on Saturday. She is only staying till Monday; she then goes to Florence.

Friday, October 7th.

Cunninghame told me that Housman has come back to London. They have got their house back. Mrs Fairburn is in London also.

Saturday, October 8th.

A. has gone down to Littlehampton.

Sunday, October 9th.

I went to see Mrs Housman in the afternoon—she was in. She leaves for Florence to-morrow. She told me she was going to stay there a whole year. She asked after A. and was pleased to hear he was still in good health. Miss Housman came in later after we had finished tea.

Letter from Guy Cunninghame to Mrs Caryl

LONDON,

Sunday, October 9th.

DEAREST ELSIE,

Thank you for your long letter. I am most worried about George. Mrs Housman goes to Florence to-morrow and is not coming back for a whole year. George has told me about the whole thing. She knows all about Housman and has always known. George has implored her to divorce Housman and to marry him. She can't divorce, as you know better than I do, and she told George it was not a marriage that could be annulled. However, this didn't satisfy him. He insisted on getting the opinion of a priest. I thought of writing to you, but there wasn't time, and then I didn't know whether it was the same in France or not. I got the opinion of a priest, who said there wasn't the slightest chance of getting the marriage annulled. I told George this and he won't believe it, even now. He keeps on saying that we ought to go to Rome, but I don't suppose that would be of the slightest use either, would it? In the meantime he is perfectly wretched. Mrs Housman didn't see him after Cornwall. George won't see anyone, or go anywhere now. He is at this moment down at Littlehampton by himself. If you can think of anything one could do, let me know at once, but I know there is nothing to be done. If the marriage could be annulled I think she would marry him to-morrow. I can't write about anything else, because I can't think about anything else.

Yrs.

G.

From the Diary of Godfrey Mellor

Monday, October 17th.

Heard from Mrs Housman from Florence. She says the weather is beautiful and she is having a very peaceful time.

Monday, November 7th.

Heard from Mrs Housman. She has been to Rome, where she stayed a fortnight.

Wednesday, November 9th.

I met Housman in the street this morning. He said he had given up the house near Staines. It was dismal in winter and not very pleasant in summer. He had taken a small house in the north of London, not far from Hendon. He could come up from there every day and the air was very good. I was not to say a word about this to Mrs Housman, as it was a surprise. He said he was going to Florence for Christmas if he could. He said I must come down one Saturday and stay with him.

Saturday, November 19th.

Staying with Riley at Shelborough.

Monday, December 12th.

Heard from Mrs Housman. She is going to spend Christmas at Ravenna with the Albertis. Housman has written to me saying he will not be able to get to Florence at Christmas and asking me to spend it with him at his house near Hendon. I have told him that I was staying with Aunt Ruth for Christmas.

Letters from Guy Cunninghame to Mrs Caryl

Monday,
October 17th.

DEAREST ELSIE,

Thank you for your letter. I quite understand all you say and I was afraid it must be so, but thank you for taking all that trouble. George is just the same. He sees nobody except Godfrey and me. I have heard from Mrs Housman twice and I have written to her several times and given her news of George. I haven't set eyes on Housman nor heard either from him or of him.

Yrs.

G.

LONDON,

Monday, October 31*st*.

DEAREST ELSIE,

I saw Jimmy Randall yesterday. He tells me that Housman is in London but has taken a house near Hendon and comes up every day. He is just, as infatuated as ever with Mrs Fairburn and has given her some handsome jewels.

I heard from Mrs Housman on Saturday. I am afraid she is quite miserable. George won't even go to stay with his sister. He dines with me sometimes.

Yrs.

G.

LONDON,

November 14*th.*

DEAREST ELSIE,

Lady Jarvis is back from Ireland. I went down to Rosedale on Saturday. There were a few people there, but I managed to have two long and good talks with her. She is of course fearfully worried. She hears from Mrs Housman constantly, she never mentions G. Lady Jarvis thinks of going out there, only, apparently, Mrs Housman will not be at Florence for Christmas. She tried to get George to come to Rosedale, but he wouldn't.

I have seen Housman for a moment at the play. He said I must see his house at Hendon. He said he had meant it as a surprise for Mrs H., but he had been obliged to tell her. He says he has bought a lot of new pictures and that the house is very *moderne* in arrangement. I can see it. He wanted me to go there next Saturday. I said I couldn't.

Yours,

G.

LONDON,

Tuesday, November 29*th*.

DEAREST ELSIE,

I am sorry to have been so bad about writing, but we have been having rather a busy time, which has been a good thing for George. I am going to stay with Lady Jarvis for Christmas. She asked George and he is going too. There is no party. He seems a little better, but he isn't really better, and he talks of giving up his job altogether and going out to Africa again. Will you choose me a small Christmas present for Lady Jarvis, something that looks nice in the box or case.

Yrs.

G.

LONDON,

Monday, December 12*th.*

DEAREST ELSIE,

Housman asked me so often to go down to Hendon that I was obliged to go last Saturday. The house is decorated entirely in the *Art Nouveau* style. There is a small spiral staircase made of metal in the drawing-room that goes nowhere. It is just a serpentine ornament. The house is the last word of hideosity, but the pictures are rather good. He gets good advice for these and never buys anything that, he thinks won't go up. It was a bachelor party, Randall, Carrington-Smith and myself. We played golf all the day, and Bridge all the evening.

He said Mrs Housman was enjoying Florence very much and that we must all go out there for Easter again.

I heard from her three days ago. She said very little, and asked after George. He never hears from her. He dines with me often.

Yrs.

G.

ROSEDALE,

Saturday, December 31*st.*

DEAREST ELSIE,

We have had rather a sad Christmas, only George and myself here, but Lady Jarvis has been too kind for words, and quite splendid with George. She has heard regularly from Mrs Housman and she thinks she will go out to Florence in January if she can.

Godfrey is staying with his uncle. Lady Jarvis says that Miss Sarah Housman makes terrible scenes about Mrs Fairburn, so much so that Sarah and he are no longer on speaking terms. I go back to London just after the New Year, so does George. The Christmas present was a great success. Lady Jarvis gave me a lovely table for my flat.

Yrs.

G.

From the Diary of Godfrey Mellor

Monday, January 2nd, 1911.

Received a small Dante bound in white vellum from Mrs Housman. It had been delayed in the post.

Tuesday, January 3rd.

Cunninghame came to the office to-day. A. also.

Tuesday, April 12th.

Riley is spending Easter in London. He wishes to attend the Holy Week services. He is staying with me.

Wednesday, April 13th.

Sat up with Riley, talking. I told him about Hope having said that he considered that to become an R.C. was to sin against the light. Riley said that Hope might very likely end by committing suicide, as views such as he held led to despair. He said: "If the Catholic religion is like what Hope and you think it to be, it must be inconceivable that anyone whose character and whose intelligence you respect could belong to such a Church, but, granting you do, does it not occur to you that it is just possible the Catholic religion may be unlike what you think it is, may indeed be something quite different?"

I said that I did not at all share Hope's views. Indeed I did not know what they were. I said that I agreed with him that when one got to know R.C.'s one found they were quite different from what they were supposed to be, and I was quite ready to believe this applied to their beliefs also.

I said something about the complication of the Catholic system, which was difficult to reconcile with the simplicity of the early Church. He said the services of the early Church were longer and more complicated than they were now. The services of the Eastern Church were more complicated than those of the Western Church, and to this day in the Coptic Church it took eight hours to say Mass. The Church was complicated when described, but simple when experienced.

Saturday, April 16th.

Went with Riley to the ceremony of the Blessing of the Font at Westminster Cathedral. Riley said he was sorry for people who had to go to Maeterlinck for symbolism.

Received a postcard from Florence. Housman did not go out after all.

Monday, May 1st.

Cunninghame told us that Housman is laid up with pneumonia.

Thursday, May 4th.

Housman is worse, and Mrs Housman has been telegraphed for. He is laid up at Hendon. They don't think he will recover.

Friday, May 5th.

Mrs Housman arrived last night. Housman is about the same.

Monday, May 8th.

Had luncheon with Lady Jarvis yesterday. She says that Housman was a shade better yesterday. He may recover, but it is thought very doubtful. Mrs Housman has been up day and night nursing him.

Wednesday, May 10th.

Housman has taken a turn for the better, but he is not yet out of danger.

Saturday, May 13th.

The doctors say Housman is out of danger.

Monday, May 15th.

Cunninghame says Housman will recover. He has been very bad indeed. The doctors say that it is entirely due to Mrs Housmans nursing that he has pulled through.

Saturday, May 20th.

Went to see Mrs Housman at Hendon. I was allowed to see Housman for a few minutes. He likes visitors. Mrs Housman looked tired. Cunninghame says that Housman has a weak heart. That was the danger.

Saturday, June 10th.

The Housmans have gone to Brighton for a fortnight.

Letters from Guy Cunninghame to Mrs Caryl

LONDON,

Monday, May 22nd.

DEAREST ELSIE,

I am delighted to hear you and Jack are coming to London so soon, but very sad of course that you won't be going back to Paris. But I believe Copenhagen is a delightful post, and they say it always leads to something.

Perhaps you will let me come and stay with you in the summer?

Yrs.

G.

Saturday, June 10th.

DEAREST ELSIE,

Your letter made me laugh a great deal. I expect you will get to like the place. I am writing this from Rosedale, where I am in the middle of a large musical and artistic party, one painter, two novelists, and two pianists. They all hate each other like poison, and it is pain to all the others when one of them performs. But the rest of us are enjoying it immensely, and Lady Jarvis is being splendid. The Housmans have gone to Brighton for a fortnight. Bert is quite well again, but Mrs Housman looks fearfully ill.

Write to me again soon.

Yrs.

G.

Monday, June 26th.

DEAREST ELSIE,

I have just come back from Oakley, the Housmans' place, near Hendon. He has quite recovered, and everything was going on there just as usual. Jimmy Randall was there, and Mrs Fairburn. Housman said nothing about the summer, but Mrs Housman told me she was not going to Cornwall this year. I asked her if she was going to stay all the summer at Oakley, the Hendon house. She said that Housman had hired a yacht for the summer and asked several people. She said she couldn't bear steam yachting with a large party, and she has taken a small house on the west coast of Ireland, with Lady Jarvis. They would be there quite alone; she was going there quite soon: "Albert would probably go to France."

She told me Housman had wanted to take the house in Cornwall and ask us all again, but that she had told him this was impossible.

George has seen her once or twice, and he is of course happier, but things are where they were. She won't think of divorcing.

I shall start for Copenhagen at the end of July.

Yrs.

G.

From the Diary of Godfrey Mellor

Tuesday, June 27th. London.

Housman has asked me to go to Oakley next Saturday. He has asked A. also.

Wednesday, June 28th. London.

Dined with A. and his sister. A. said he would be unable to go to Oakley next week. He had some people staying with him.

Thursday, June 29th. London.

Dined with Aunt Ruth. Apparently Gertrude is still annoyed at the Caryls having got Copenhagen. She complains of this weekly.

Friday, June 30th. London.

Solway is staying the night with me, his concert is to-morrow afternoon.

Saturday, July 1st. London.

Went with Mrs Housman to Solway's concert in the afternoon, and she drove me down to Hendon afterwards in her motor. Mrs Housman is going to spend the summer in Ireland.

Sunday, July 2nd. Oakley (near Hendon).

Mrs Fairburn and Carrington-Smith are staying here. Mrs Housman leaves to-morrow for Ireland.

Saturday, October 28th. London, Gray's Inn.

Mrs Housman returns from Ireland to-day. She spends Sunday in London, and goes to Oakley, near Hendon, on Wednesday. I have not heard one word from Mrs Housman since her long absence in Ireland.

Sunday, October 29th.

Went to see Mrs Housman in the afternoon. Ireland has done her a great deal of good, and she looks quite refreshed and rested.

She asked after A. I told her he was due to arrive from Scotland to-morrow, and that we expected him at the office. She asked me if I was going to stay with Lady Jarvis next Saturday. She said we would meet there. She said nothing about her plans for the future.

Monday, October 30th.

A. has arrived from Scotland, and Cunninghame from Copenhagen, where he has been staying for the last three months with his cousin. I called on Lady Jarvis. She told me she thought Mrs Housman would not remain long in England. She might go to Italy again.

Tuesday, October 31st.

A. is going to Rosedale on Saturday.

Wednesday, November 1st.

Dined with A. and Cunninghame. We went to a music hall after dinner.

Thursday, November 2nd.

Cunninghame and I went to Aunt Ruth's after dinner. When Cunninghame said he had been at Copenhagen, Aunt Ruth said that she knew, of course, Caryl was a brilliant diplomatist, but that Edmund Anstruther ought to have had the post. Uncle Arthur said: "What, Edmund? Copenhagen? He would have got us into war with the Danes."

Friday, November 3rd.

Dined alone with A. He asked after Mrs Housman's health.

Saturday, November 4th. Rosedale.

A.. Cunninghame, myself, and Mrs Vaughan are here. The Housmans were unable to come at the last moment.

Monday, November 6th.

Housman asked me to go to Oakley on Saturday, November 25th. Mrs Housman has gone to Folkestone for a fortnight to stay with Miss Housman. Cunninghame says that Housman and his sister have quarrelled, and that she no longer goes to the house.

Saturday, November 25th. Oakley.

Lady Jarvis, A. and Carrington-Smith are staying here. Cunninghame comes down to-morrow for the day. Housman was obliged to go to Paris on urgent business for a few days.

Sunday, November 26th.

Cunninghame and Carrington-Smith played golf. I went for a walk with Lady Jarvis.

Monday, November 27th.

Dined with A. and went to the play, a farce. A. enjoyed it immensely. I have written to Aunt Ruth to tell her I shall not be able to go there this year. I shall remain in London, as Riley wishes to spend Christmas with me.

Tuesday, November 28th.

Dined with Lady Jarvis. Mrs Housman has gone back to Folkestone. She stays there till Christmas, then she returns to London.

A. is going abroad for Christmas.

Wednesday, December 20th.

A. goes to Paris to-morrow night. Cunninghame is going to spend Christmas with the Housmans at Oakley.

Letter from Guy Cunninghame to Mrs Caryl

HALKIN STREET,

Friday, December 22nd.

DEAREST ELSIE,

As you see, I write from London. All my plans have been upset by an unexpected catastrophe. I will try and begin at the beginning and tell you everything in order as clearly as possible, but the fact is I am so bewildered by everything that has happened that I find it difficult to think clearly and to write at all.

I think I told you in my last letter that Housman asked me to spend Christmas with them at Oakley. I was to go down yesterday, Thursday, and George was going to Paris by the night train. I think I told you, too, that ever since we stayed at Oakley in November, George has been a *changed man* and in the highest spirits. On Thursday we had luncheon together. I thought it rather odd that he should be going to Paris, but he said he was tired of England and felt that he must have a change. I wondered what this meant. I could have imagined his wanting to go away if he had been like he was before, that is to say miserable, but now that he seemed to be enjoying life it was rather extraordinary. I said I was going to Oakley. He said nothing, and talked about his journey. After luncheon he went to the office to give Mellor some final instructions. He said he might be away for some time. I left him there at about half-past three. I asked him why he was going by the night train, and he said he hated a day in the train and always slept well in the train at night. I said good-bye and went down to Oakley in a taxi. Housman had not arrived, and the butler (who has taken the place of the nice parlour-maid there used to be at Campden Hill) told me that Mrs Housman had gone up to London. Her maid thought she was staying the night at Garland's Hotel, but he, the butler, knew nothing of her arrangements. This astonished me, but I supposed there were no servants at Campden Hill. At a quarter to five Housman arrived in a motor with Carrington-Smith. He looked more yellow than usual. I met him in the hall and while we were talking the butler gave him a letter which he said Mrs Housman had left for him. He said we would have tea at once in the drawing-room. Then he said to Carrington-Smith: "I just want to show you that thing," and to me: "We will be with you in one minute." He took Carrington-Smith into his study and I went into the drawing-room. Tea was brought in. I again tried the butler and asked him whether Mrs Housman was coming back to-morrow morning. He said that she had left no instructions, but Mr Housman was probably aware of her intentions. He went out and almost directly I heard someone shouting and bells ringing, violently. Carrington-Smith was calling me. I ran out and met him in the hall; he said Housman had had a stroke, he thought it was fatal.

It was like a thing on the stage. A breathless telephone to the doctor. The motor sent to fetch him. Servants scurrying with blanched faces.

Housman lying on the sofa in the study, his collar undone, his face ghastly.

Carrington-Smith said: "We must telephone to Campden Hill for Mrs Housman."

I said: "She isn't there." Then told him about Garland's Hotel. He seemed *dumbfounded,* sent for the butler, who confirmed this, and then got on to the Hotel. Mrs Housman was in. He spoke to her and told her Housman was dangerously ill and she must come at once. He said he would get on to Miss Housman and tell her to bring Mrs Housman down in her motor. This was arranged and he told Miss Housman the whole facts. In the meantime the doctor arrived—an Australian. He examined Housman and said it was heart failure and that he had always feared this. They had known he had a weak heart after his last illness. It might have happened any day.

Then Carrington-Smith told me how it had happened. When they went into the study Housman had sat down at his writing-table and read a letter through twice quite slowly, torn it up and thrown it into the fire. He had then said: "We will go," and at that moment fallen back and collapsed on the sofa.

He told me that Housman had had a terrific row with Mrs Fairburn yesterday and had talked of nothing else on the way down. Probably the letter was from her, he said. I said: "Yes, very likely"; but as a matter of fact I knew it was from Mrs Housman. He had not noticed that, or if he had he was lying on purpose.

Mrs Housman and Miss Housman arrived about six. Mrs Housman almost *frighteningly* calm.

She wanted to know every detail. She had a talk with Carrington-Smith alone and then I saw her for a moment before going away. She asked me if I had seen Housman before he died. Then she made all the arrangements herself. I went back to London by train.

I don't know what to think. Why did she go to London? Why did she stay at Garland's Hotel? The Campden Hill house isn't shut up. Miss Housman talked about going there. Did the letter which she left for Housman play a part in the tragedy?

I sent George a telegram. Possibly you may see him.

Yours,

G.

From the Diary of Godfrey Mellor

Friday, December 22nd.

I was rung up last night by Cunninghame, who had returned to London unexpectedly. He had bad news to tell me. A tragedy had occurred at Oakley and Housman had died suddenly of a heart attack. Mrs Housman was informed at once and reached Oakley an hour after the tragedy occurred.

Cunninghame has informed A. by telegram.

Not unconnected with this tragic event a small incident has occurred to me which leaves me stunned.

I have unwittingly violated A.'s confidence, and as it were looked through a keyhole into his private affairs. I am literally appalled by what I have done. But after reviewing every detail and living again every moment of yesterday, I do not see how I could have acted otherwise than I did, nor do I see how things could have happened differently.

These are the facts:

A. arrived at the office at half-past three on Thursday afternoon with Cunninghame. Cunninghame left him.

A. remained in his room until five o'clock, writing letters.

At five he sent for me and told me he was leaving for Paris that night by the night train. Tuke, he said, had gone on his holiday. He asked me if I was going away. I said I should be in London during all the Christmas holidays, as I had a friend staying with me. He said he would most probably be away for some time, and he would be obliged if I could look in at the office every now and then. He had told the clerks to forward letters, but he wanted me to make sure they did not forward circulars or any other useless documents to him. I was to open all telegrams, whether private or not, and not to forward them unless they were of real importance. "But," he said, "there won't be any telegrams. Don't forward me invitations to luncheon or dinner."

This morning I went to the office. There was a telegram for A. The clerk gave it to me. I opened it. It had been sent off originally at five yesterday afternoon and redirected from Stratton Street. Its contents were: "Albert dangerously ill. Fear worst. Cannot come. Clare."

I forwarded it to the Hôtel Meurice. He will know of course that I have read it. I read it at one glance before I realised its nature. Then it was too late. And so unwittingly I am guilty of the greatest breach of confidence that I could possibly have committed.

It was a fatality that this telegram should have missed him. The clerks say he left the office soon after I did, a little after five. They say the telegram did not reach the office till later. They didn't know where A. was and he had told them not to forward any telegrams till I had seen them. I remember his saying that he was not returning to his flat. That he was dining at a club and going straight from thereto the station, where his servant would meet him. I am truly appalled by what I have done, but the more I think over it, the less I see how it could have been otherwise.

I had some conversation with Cunninghame on the telephone last night. He had been talking to Lady Jarvis on the telephone. She had at once offered to go to Oakley, but Mrs Housman said she would rather see no one at present.

Cunninghame went down to Rosedale at her urgent request this morning. He did not call at the office on the way.

Letters from Guy Cunninghame to Mrs Caryl

ROSEDALE,

Friday, December 22nd.

DEAREST ELSIE,

I came down here early this morning. Lady Jarvis heard the news from Miss Housman last night and at once offered to go, but Mrs Housman said she would rather see no one at present. Carrington-Smith was making all the arrangements. The funeral is to be on Tuesday. I told Lady Jarvis about Mrs Housman being in London. She said Mrs Housman often went up to Garland's Hotel. She found it a complete rest and the house at Campden Hill was very cold and there was no cook there. Lady Jarvis said it was the most natural thing in the world. I told her about the letter. She said Mrs Housman had no doubt written to Housman saying she had gone to Garland's Hotel and was coming back. I also told her what Carrington-Smith had said about Mrs Fairburn. She said: "That was it. It was those terrible scenes which used to shatter him and no doubt caused his death." Lady Jarvis says it will be a shock to Mrs Housman in spite of everything. The fact of Housman having made her very unhappy, or rather of her having been very unhappy as his wife, will make no difference to the shock. Lately Lady Jarvis says he had made things very difficult for her. Mrs Fairburn was always there.

One can't help thinking—well you know, I needn't explain. I wonder what will happen in the future. I have heard nothing from George yet. There is no one here. Housman must have left an enormous fortune. He was very canny about his investments, and very lucky too. Randall told me he had almost doubled his fortune in the last three years, and he was rich enough to start with.

Yours,

G.

P.S..—Lady Jarvis' explanation of the letter does not quite satisfy, but what *did* happen? What does it all mean?

LONDON,

Monday, January 1*st*.

DEAREST ELSIE,

I came up to-day for good. I went to Housman's funeral last Tuesday. Mrs Housman went down to Rosedale directly after the funeral. She is going to Florence next week and means to stay on there indefinitely. George has come back. He never wrote and I did not hear from him till he arrived at the office this morning. He is just the same as usual except for being subtly different.

Housman left everything to her.

Yrs.

G.

P.S.—I told Godfrey everything that had happened at Oakley. He said *nothing*. He appears incapable of discussing the matter.

From the Diary of Godfrey Mellor

Monday, January 1*st*, 1912.

A. arrived last night from Paris. He came to the office and he thanked me for what I had done in his absence. "Everything was quite right," he said. He conveyed to me without saying anything that I need not distress myself about the telegram and that he still trusted me.

He did not mention Mrs Housman nor the death of Housman.

Wednesday, February 28*th*.

I heard to-day from Mrs Housman. She tells me she has entered the Convent of the Presentation and intends to be a nun. I cannot say the news surprised me, but to hear of the death in life of anyone one knows well, is almost worse I think than to hear of their death.

Letter from Guy Cunninghame to Mrs Caryl

LONDON,

Wednesday, February 28*th*.

DEAREST ELSIE,

I have just had a short letter from Lady Jarvis telling me that Mrs Housman is going to be a nun. I have not set eyes on her since Housmans funeral, and have only heard of her, and that not much, from time to time from Lady Jarvis.

I confess I am completely bewildered, and I hope you won't be shocked if I tell you that I' can't help thinking it rather *selfish*. Do as I will, I cannot see any possible reason for her taking such a step. Mrs Housman seems to me the last person in the world who ought to be a nun. Whether it will make her happy or not, I am afraid there is no doubt that she will be causing a lot of intense misery. George is worse than ever. He hasn't in the least got over it, and he never will, I feel sure. He knows what has happened, but he can't even bring himself to talk about it. I think he must have known of it for some time. In any case he hasn't for one moment emerged from the real fog of gloom and misery that has wrapped him up ever since Christmas.

What is so extraordinary is that just before Christmas he was in radiant spirits after all those months of sadness!

I can't see that it *can* be right, however good the motive, to destroy and shatter someone's life!

His life *is* destroyed, shattered and shipwrecked! We must just face that.

I tried to think that we had always been wrong and that my first impressions were right, that she had never really cared for him. But I know this is not true. You will forgive me saying that I think your religion has a terribly hard and cruel side. Nobody appreciates more than I do all its good points, and nobody knows better than I do what a lot of good is often done by Catholics. But it is just this sort of thing that makes one *revolt*.

I was reading Boswell last night before going to bed, and I came across this sentence: "Madam," Dr Johnson said, to a nun in a convent, "you are here not from love of virtue, but from fear of vice." Even this is not a satisfactory explanation in Mrs Housmans case. It is obvious that she had nothing to fear from vice. I can't help thinking she has been the victim of an inexorable system and of a training which bends the human mind into a twisted shape that can never be altered or put straight.

Frankly, I think it is *more* than sad, I think it is positively *wicked*; not on her part, but on the part of those who have led her to take such a mistaken view of ordinary human duty. After all, even if she wants to be a nun, isn't it her duty to stay in the world? Isn't it a more difficult duty? What is one's duty to one's neighbour? Forgive me for saying all this. You know in my case that it isn't inspired by prejudice.

It is cruel to think that most probably George will never get over this, and that she has sacrificed the certain happiness of two human beings and the chance of doing any amount of good in the world. What for? For nothing as far as I can see that can't be much better done by people far more fitted to that kind of vocation. I am too sad to write any more.

Yrs.

G.

From the Diary of Godfrey Mellor

Thursday, March 1st.

I dined alone with Cunninghame at his flat last night. He had heard the news about Mrs Housman. He was greatly upset about it, and thought it very selfish. I said I believed the step was not irrevocable, as one had to stay some time in a convent before taking final vows.

He said: "That is just what I want to talk about, just what I want to know. How long must one stay exactly?"

I said I did not know, but I could find out. He said I want you to find out all about it as soon as possible. A., he said, was in a dreadful state. He had dined with him last night. He had said very little; nothing personal, not a word about what he felt about it, but he had asked him, Cunninghame, whether he knew what the rules were about taking the veil.

C. said he did not believe Mrs Housman would take an irrevocable decision. He had told A. he would find out all about it. I could of course ask Riley, but I don't know whether he would know.

I decided I would apply to Father Stanway, the priest I met at Carbis Bay, for information. I wrote to him, saying I wished to consult him on a matter, and suggested going down to Cornwall on Saturday and spending Sunday at Carbis Bay.

Friday, March 2nd.

Received a telegram from Father Stanway, saying that he will not be in Cornwall this week-end, but in London, where he will be staying four or five days; and suggesting our meeting on Sunday afternoon. I sent him a telegram asking him to luncheon on Sunday.

Sunday, March 4th.

Father Stanway came to luncheon with me at the Club, and we talked of the topics of the day. After luncheon I suggested a walk in the park. We went for a walk in Kensington Gardens. I asked him first for the information about the nuns. He said, as far as he could say off-hand, it entailed six months' postulancy, two years' "Habit and White Veil," three years' *simple* vows of profession; and then solemn perpetual vows. But he said he could write to a convent and get it quite accurate for me. In any case he knew it was a matter of five years.

I then said I would like, if he did not mind, to have his opinion on a case which I had come across. He said he would be pleased to listen.

I then told him the whole Housman story as a skeleton case, not mentioning names, and calling the people X. and Y. Very possibly he knew who I was talking about, almost certainly I think, although he never betrayed this for a moment. I felt the knowledge, if there were knowledge, would be as safe as though given in the confessional. I told him everything, including a detailed account of Housman's death which Cunninghame had given me. I referred to Housman as X., to Mrs Housman as Mrs X. and to A. as Y.

I then asked him if he thought Mrs X. was justified in taking such a step, and whether it would not be nobler, a more unselfish course, to remain in the world and to make Y. happy.

I asked him whether, in his opinion, people would be justified in calling Mrs X.'s step, were it to turn out to be irrevocable, a *selfish* act.

And, thirdly, I asked if in the case of Mrs X. changing her mind she would be allowed by the Church to marry Y.

Father Stanway said if I wished to understand the question I must try and turn my mind round, as it were, and start from the point of view that what the world considers all-important the Church considers of no importance *if it interferes with what God thinks important*. He said I must start by remembering that Mrs X.'s conduct proceeded from that idea—what was important in the eyes of God: she believed in God *practically* and not merely theoretically. This belief was the cardinal fact and the compass of her life. He added that this did not mean the Church was unsympathetic. No one understood human nature as well as she did, nobody met it as she did at every point. That was why she helped it to rise superior to its weakness and to do what it saw to be really best. He said it was no disgrace to be weak, and vows helped one to do what might be difficult without them.

Then he said that if Mrs X. felt she was called to the religious life, this vocation was the result of supernatural Grace; that she would not be thinking of what was delightful or convenient to her, but of what was pleasing and honourable to God. She was bound to follow the appointment of God, if she felt certain that was His appointment, rather than her own desire, and before anything she desired.

Here I said the objection made (and I quoted Cunninghame without mentioning him) was that her desire might be for the calm and security of the religious life; but might it not be her duty, possibly a more difficult, a more unselfish and less pleasant duty, to stay in the world and not to shatter the happiness of another human being?

Father Stanway then said it was very easy to delude oneself in most things, but not in following a religious vocation. One might in *not* following it. It would be easy to pretend to oneself one was staying in the world for someone else's sake. One's merely earthly happiness was not a reason for *not* following a vocation, nor was anyone else's, because the religious life belonged not to things temporal but to things eternal. However, if it were her duty to remain in the world she would feel no call to leave the world. It was impossible for a human being to gauge the vocation of another human being. A vocation was a "categorical imperative" to the soul, and there was no mistaking its presence. Mrs X. would know for certain after she had spent some time in the Convent, she probably knew already, whether or no what she felt was a vocation or not. Nobody else could judge, though her Director might help her to decide. He would certainly not allow her to stay if he felt she had no vocation.

I said: "So, if after she has lived through her first period, or any period of probation, she feels uncertain as to her vocation, there would be no objection to her leaving the religious life, and marrying Y.? Would the Church then allow her to marry Y., and allow her to go back to the world, knowing she would in all probability marry Y.?"

Father Stanway said: "Of course, and the Church would allow her to marry Y. now."

I said, perhaps a little impatiently: "Then why doesn't she?"

"I think," said Father Stanway, "you are a musician, Mr Mellor?"

I said music was my one and sole hobby.

He said he would try and express himself in terms of harmony.

"Perhaps Mrs X. has a great sense of harmony herself," he said. "If she married Y. that would make a legitimate harmony certainly. But her very feeling for the *full* harmony of life would make it impossible" (and he said this with startling emphasis) "*for her to use X.'s death as a means for doing rightly what she had meant to do wrongly*, for her intention to do it wrongly had in a measure caused his death. Within the harmony of her marriage the memory of that discord would always be present. And perhaps she is a woman who is able to have a vision of perfect love and harmony. In that case she could not put up with an imperfect one. She is now free to enter upon a perfect harmony and love, by marrying Christ, which I imagine she always wanted to do, even in the normal married state, in fact by means of the normal married state, for it is a Sacrament and unites the soul to God by Grace.

"But I understand from you that her marriage was such a travesty of marriage that she felt she couldn't worship Christ through that, and so swung across and decided she couldn't be in relation with Him at all. Then comes this catastrophe and the pendulum swings back and stops up.

"There is nothing selfish about this. For all we know it was the will of God that all this should happen (the shipwreck of her marriage, Y.'s love and present misery) solely to make her vocation certain, and as far as Y. is concerned we don't know the end. Even from the worldly point of view we don't know whether his marriage with Mrs X. would have made for his ultimate happiness or for hers. His present unhappiness may be an essential note in the full and total harmony of *his* life. It may be a beginning and not an end. It may lead him to some eventual happiness, it may be welding his nature and his life for some undreamed-of purpose, a purpose which he may afterwards be led to recognise and bless 'with tears of recognition.' If Mrs X. is certain of her vocation, and continues to be certain of it, you can be sure she is right, and that whatever the world says it will be wrong.

"The only way in which peace comes to the human soul is in accepting the will of God, 'In la sua volontate e nostra pace.'

"Mrs X. knows that, and perhaps Y. is on the road to learning it. I daresay Mrs X. may have an element of fear of life *too*, but it will thin out and float off and away from her; her act in choosing the religious life will not be an escape nor a *flight*, but a positive acceptance of the love of Christ. She is getting to and at the mysterious spiritual thing which is in music, and which is as different from sounds as sounds are different from printed notes. It is you musicians who know."

I said that although I did not pretend to understand the whole thing, and the whole nature of the motive, I could understand that it could be as he said, and I thanked him, telling him that I for one should never cavil at her act nor criticise it, but always understand that there was something to understand, although probably it would always be beyond my understanding.

I felt during all this conversation that the real problem was not why she had become a nun, but what terrible thing had happened inside her mind to make her take that step at Christmas, and decide on what seemed to contradict all her life so far.

I said something about religion not affecting conduct in a crisis. Father Stanway seemed to read my thoughts. He said: "After a long stress sometimes a tiny accident will suffice to make a nerve snap *suddenly*. I should say that in this case long stress had pushed and pushed a soul out of its real shape and pattern; an unknown factor sufficed to force it into a coherent but false pattern; a new shock sufficed to liberate it wholly and let it fall back into its original *true* pattern. That may account for half of it."

Wednesday, March 7th.

I dined alone with Cunninghame last night, and told him what I had ascertained respecting the rules for the period of probation of nuns. He appeared to be relieved. I warned him that Mrs Housman's step might very well prove to be irrevocable, as I didn't think she was a person to change her mind easily. He said: "That's what I am afraid of. They never do let people go. I feel that once in a convent they will never let her go. But it will be a relief to A. to know that the step is not yet irrevocable."

Letters from Guy Cunninghame to Mrs Caryl

LONDON,

Wednesday, March 7th.

DEAREST ELSIE,

Godfrey dined with me last night. I feel he thinks that Mrs Housmans step will be irrevocable, although he didn't actually say so. He said he didn't pretend to understand it, but he was convinced she knew best. I talked of George's acute misery. He said it was all very difficult to understand, and I saw he didn't want to discuss it, so I didn't say any more. I feel he knows something that we don't know, but what? He told me that he knew on good authority that going into Convent doesn't mean she takes the veil for five years. An R.C. who knows all about it had told him. I suppose this is right? Do ask a priest. I have seen George once or twice. I don't talk about it to him. In fact, the rules about nuns is the only point that has been mentioned between us as I see he simply can't talk about it. He looks ten years older.

Yours,

G.

LONDON,

Monday, March 12th.

DEAREST ELSIE,

Thank you very much for your letter and for the detailed information. I told George at once that you had confirmed what Godfrey had said, and he was really relieved. But he doesn't yet look like a man who has had a *reprieve*, only a respite.

I feel that he feels it is all over, but personally I shall go on hoping.

Lady Jarvis is away.

I long to talk about it with her.

Yours,

G.

From the Diary of Godfrey Mellor

Sunday, August 19*th. Rosedale.*

I am staying with Lady Jarvis. There is no one here but myself and Cunninghame. She told us she had heard from Mrs Housman, who has finished her postulancy and received the novice's white veil.

She had seen her. She says she is quite certain that it is irrevocable and that Mrs Housman will never change her mind now.

Cunninghame said he had hoped up till now this would not happen (though he had always feared it might happen) and that Mrs Housman would think better of it. He thought it very wrong and selfish and quite inexcusable on the part of the Church authorities.

Lady Jarvis said it must appear so to him. She herself would have no sympathy with a vocation such as this one must appear to be to the world in general, and even to people who knew Mrs Housman well, like Cunninghame and myself; so Mrs Housman's act had not surprised her.

"But," said Cunninghame, "do you approve of it?"

"The person concerned," said Lady Jarvis, "is the only judge in such a matter. Nobody else has the right to judge. It's a sacred thing, and the approval or disapproval of an outsider is I think simply impertinent."

We then talked of it no more. But in the afternoon I went out for a walk with Lady Jarvis and she reverted to the question.

She said: "I hope you understand I'm so far from disapproving of Clare's act. I understand it and approve of it; but I don't expect you or anyone else to do the same."

I said she need not have told me that. I knew it already.

She then said: "Clare knew you would understand, even if you didn't understand."

I said that was my exact position: "I did not understand, but I knew there was something to understand, and that therefore she was right."

Letter from Guy Cunninghame to Mrs Caryl

LONDON,

Monday, August 10*th.*

DEAREST ELSIE,

I have just come back from Rosedale. There is no one there except Godfrey. Lady Jarvis told us that Mrs Housman has finished the first period you told me about, and has taken the veil, though it isn't irrevocable yet, but for all intents and purposes it is, as we are all certain now that she will never leave the Convent. You know what I think about it. I haven't changed my mind, but Lady Jarvis doesn't disapprove, or is too loyal to say so.

George knows, he is going to Ireland with his sister.

I can't help thinking it is all a great, a wicked mistake, and I can't help still thinking it *selfish*.

George talked about Mrs Housman, at least he just alluded to her having become a nun, as if it were a fact and quite irrevocable. He said: "Once the priests get hold of someone they will never let them go, and in this case it was a regular conspiracy." But somehow or other this did not seem to me to ring quite true, from *him*, and I felt he was using this as a shield or a disguise or mask. I said so to Godfrey, but found it impossible to get any response. He won't talk about it.

Yours,

G.

From the Diary of Godfrey Mellor

Sunday, August 26th. Carbis Bay Hotel.

I have come down here to spend a week by myself. It is three years ago since I came here for the first time to stay with Mr and Mrs Housman.

I hesitated about coming down here again, but I am now glad that I did so.

I went to Father Stanway's church this morning and heard him preach. He is a good preacher, clear and unaffected. He quoted two sayings which struck me. One was about going away from earthly solace, and the other I cannot remember well enough to transcribe, but I have written him a post card asking who said them and where I could find them.

In the afternoon I went for a walk alone along the cliffs and passed the place where we began *Les Misérables*. I am re-reading it, not where we left off, but from the beginning.

Monday, August 27th.

Father Stanway called this morning while I was out. He has left me the quotations on a card.

They are both from Thomas à Kempis. One of them is this: "By so much the more does a man draw nigh to God as he goes away from all earthly solace." The other: "Whosoever is not ready to suffer all things and to stand resigned to the will of his beloved is not worthy to be called a lover."

Tuesday, August 28th.

I have resolved to give up keeping this diary.

THE END

Printed in Dunstable, United Kingdom

73974284R00068